# CHARLES HALDEMAN

## A MEMOIR; MIDCENTURY JOURNEYS OF A VAGABOND AUTHOR

## RICHARD HALDEMAN

# CHARLES HALDEMAN

## *A MEMOIR; MIDCENTURY JOURNEYS OF A VAGABOND AUTHOR*

## RICHARD HALDEMAN

Kravitz & Sons

INNOVATORS IN PUBLISHING, MARKETING AND ADVERTISING

Kravitz and Sons LLC
1301 Farmville Blvd, Suite 104
Greenville, NC 27834



Published by Kravitz and Sons LLC.

ISBN:       979-8-89639-334-4 (sc)
ISBN:       979-8-89639-333-7 (e)

Library of Congress Control Number: 2025913814

Charles Haldeman
A Memoir; Midcentury Journeys of a
Vagabond Author

Richard Haldeman

# Table Of Contents

For Alexandra, Séamas, and Neil, and all those
Charles loved and who loved him

Charles Haldeman's first novel, *The Sun's Attendant,* includes an argument against publishing the letters of a deceased writer. Barbara Speer, widow of the poet Paul Speer, was organizing his letters for possible publication. Her professor friend, Karl-Heinz Hardenfield, explains why he is denying her his correspondence with Paul: "I am not refusing you these letters—I am refusing the use of them to the world. I am of the belief that every great artist bears within himself the seeds of a great man. But (perhaps only in our epoch) these seeds may flourish only in his art, only there may such a man transform, immortalize his human suffering and transcend it."

In organizing my brother's letters for this memoir, I confronted this argument that an author should be remembered only through his art. As I read Charles Haldeman's correspondence, however, counterarguments emerged: What if the writer's letters are elements of his art? What if his life itself frames elements of a novel, combining mystery, tragedy, settings worldwide, and the history and flavor of a bygone era that sowed the seeds of today's world? What if the characters in this "novel" represent the literary elite of his era?

Charles Haldeman lived a short but remarkable life, lasting from Depression to Cold War, from Herbert Hoover to Ronald Reagan, from Hitler and Stalin to Khomeini and Hussein. His life encompassed three major wars and the reconstitution of world geography and government. He lived throughout the United States—south to north, East Coast to West Coast, in big cities and small villages. He spent six months of his childhood in Hitler's Germany, sailed the Pacific in the US Navy, and lived his adult life in Germany and Greece. He was fluent in three languages in addition to his native English. He was a talented graphic and literary artist with three published novels. He wrote lyrics for the title song of an American film, the book and lyrics for a musical performed in Greece, and the scripts for award-winning documentaries. He edited a monthly history magazine. The seeds of his greatness did flourish in his art, but before and after his success as a novelist, Charles expressed in his letters his understanding of human suffering, the need not only to live but also to endure.

As the brother who knew Charles longest, I blended my earliest experiences with him with family letters and Charles's own early memories to describe his childhood and adolescence. To write about his adult years, I relied on his correspondence with those who knew him best then. To make this his memoir, I wrote in the third person. Most persons named in this memoir are now deceased, but I am thankful to Alexandra Fiada and Séamas Carraher and to my brother Neil for providing personal assistance, providing information, and setting chronology straight.

Richard H. Haldeman

Pure Gaelic blood and German forest blood:
our generation is rooted in war…
—from "Lamentations for Charles Haldeman" by Peter Levi, *Agenda*
(1984)

# PART ONE

# A Family Odyssey 1930–50

# 1
# PRELUDE

The twenty-one-year-old South Carolina woman opened the envelope in her New York City YWCA apartment and began to read the five-page letter she had received from the young German immigrant she had met only three days before.

Place: 51 Madison Avenue, New York City
Time: September 23, 1930
Scene: A lonely Dutchman sitting in his office over a blank piece of paper after a day that seemed like a week.

Hello Dearest

This certainly has been a long day for me and it is only good that I do not have to prepare any important statement these days for I could not guarantee as to their correctness. You certainly have been on my mind today Dear and if your ears were ringing every time I thought of you, you would be deaf my now...I earnestly think of beginning to count the days of my life from the day I met you (am therefore three days old and don't I act it?).

You remember Greta Garbo saying to the Count in the picture that she found something worthwhile living for in life, something she never knew of being there. I always knew that there must be something great in life and I am more than thankful to have met it in you. Honestly Dear you have that unspoiled freshness of a soul and mind which makes people coming in contact with you happy. How beautiful these last two days have been and how happy your radiant presence makes me only I know.

Only a few days ago I did not even know that there is a lovely girl called Frances in this small town and already now I would give everything I have to prevent losing her. You are already part of my life dear Frances and where it takes others months and years to gain my friendship, you have mine and myself for keeps.

The letter continued with a lament that he must cope with work and she with studies that night, but it was clear that the die had already been cast for these two romantic young people. By the end of October, they had written Frances's parents and received consent to marry, despite concern about their not having met him, his German citizenship, and her youth and innocence. On November 26, 1930, Charles Heuss and Frances McFall were married in the Church of the Transfiguration, the "Little Church Around the Corner," in New York City. Only a friend of Charles and Frances's sister, Rosa, were attendants.

Frances McFall was a descendant of Scottish and Welsh families that had migrated to America well before the Revolution. Her grandfather, Waddy McFall, was a longtime mayor of Pickens, a town in Upstate South Carolina at the edge of the Blue Ridge Mountains. Her father, Frank McFall, was president of the Pickens Bank. Her mother, Pearl Smith McFall, was an aspiring historian and author who later wrote histories of the upstate area. Her paternal grandmother, Vesta Mauldin McFall, was one of nine Mauldin siblings—male and female—to complete college and to contribute to the growth of Pickens, seat of a county created after the Civil War. Frances had attended Southern College in Petersburg, Virginia, a two-year women's college, before her father sent her to New York to study stenography at the beginning of the Depression.

Though only twenty-eight years old, Charles Heuss had already experienced several upheavals of the early twentieth century. After a happy childhood as one of six children of a locomotive engineer in (then German) Alsace-Lorraine, as a teenager he was deported with his German family by the French to Heidelberg after World War I. Trained as an accountant, Charles (then Karl) coped as a banker with post–World War I inflation in Germany. In 1926 he migrated to the United States to work for the Smith & Corona Typewriter Company in New York City. Sadly, his father died the year he migrated, and Charles was unable to keep his promise to his mother that he would return to Germany as he advanced rapidly over the next four years to a chief accountancy position with Smith-Corona.

Charles and Frances began their married life at a home on Long Island. On September 27, 1931, their first son, Charles Frank Heuss, was born in Pickens where Frances had returned for the birth. In 1933, Charles, Frances, and little Charles moved to Syracuse, New York, where Smith-Corona had relocated. Charles and Frances were visited by her parents; younger sister, Vesta; and brother, Waddy, in Syracuse the following year. By 1934 Smith-Corona was emerging from company struggles caused by its move to Syracuse, lessening the stress of Charles Heuss's work. In February 1934 he gained American citizenship at about the same time Frances discovered she was expecting again. Charles and Frances welcomed a second son, Richard, on October 24, 1934, a month after little Charles's third birthday.

Charles and Frances sent affectionate and humorous cards to one another during this time, indicating their continued deep love for one another; and they took several photos of little Charles holding baby Richard. The year 1935 dawned happily for the Heuss family: the family now included two little boys and two loving parents; their home in Syracuse included good friends and neighbors; Smith-Corona was beginning to thrive; and Charles Heuss had gained American citizenship in 1934, just after Hitler had come into power in his native Germany.

Within three months, however, Frances and her two boys would find their lives altered forever. In March Charles Heuss fell ill with a strep infection. His condition would have been curable by penicillin only a few years later, but his condition worsened; and on March 25, 1935, he died.

At twenty-five years old, Frances McFall Heuss was a widow with two little boys hundreds of miles from her South Carolina home.

These were to be the first memories of little Charles, three-and-a-half years old.

II

# A South Carolina Interlude and a Visit to Germany

Frances McFall Heuss had only a kind condolence letter from Smith-Corona president Hurlbut W. Smith, assistance from friends and family, and payment of a $50-per-month life insurance policy from her husband to assist her in the move from Syracuse to her parents' home in Pickens. She brought with her the remains of her husband, to be buried in the McFall family plot in Sunrise Cemetery in Pickens. His tombstone reads "Charles Heuss; May 17, 1902–March 25, 1935; 'Du lebst auch in der heimat fort denn liebe reichet uber's meer!'" ("You live on also in the homeland, for love reaches over the sea!").

It became Frances's intention to carry her love "over the sea" to Charles's family in Germany. Fortunately, Germany was presenting its best face to the world in 1935 as it planned to host the Olympic Games the following year. With assistance from her father, Frank McFall, Frances made plans to travel to Germany with her two children from September 1935 to February 1936. Frances was fortunate that in the midst of the Depression, her father had a secure position and salary, the Pickens Bank having survived the crash to become a wing of the South Carolina National Bank. In a South still suffering seventy years later from the effects of Civil War, the McFalls lived a comfortable life in a spacious two-story home with acres of property.

Little Charles ("Charlie") was able to roam the woods behind the home with his Uncle Waddy. Waddy was the youngest of four children and the only son of Frank and Pearl Smith McFall. From his earliest childhood, he had been a naturalist, freely wandering the surrounding mountains to study its animals and plants. He had dropped out of The Citadel and Clemson because their military cultures restricted

4

his freedom. He had a natural gift for painting and taught himself taxidermy. His nephew Charlie was able to view the many paintings and trophies he kept in his private shed behind the family home. (Later Waddy received training from the American Museum of Natural History in New York, working there and helping to prepare the models of North American mammals in the years before World War II. This led to a distinguished career as a game warden and taxidermist.)

Frank McFall also doted over Charlie and his little brother, Richard (known to his family as Dicky), spending hours playing with them in the living room and yard. He became a surrogate father to both Charlie, who had faint memories of his own father, and Dicky, who loved to line up chairs in the living room to play "train" with his grandfather. The children were taken swimming and floated toy boats at Table Rock and Rocky Bottom Parks nearby.

Charlie and Dicky Heuss grew up in a Pickens that included a myriad of grandparents, aunts, uncles, and cousins they knew only as "Gramma and Grandpa" (their grandparents), "Ivy's Mammy" and "Ivy" (their great grandmother and special-needs great aunt), "Aunt Queen" (their great aunt and DAR lady), "Lee and Jess," "Aunt Jo," "Aunt Vesta and Uncle Red," "Aunt Rosa and Uncle Bill," and "May and Ora." An African American couple, "Mame and Babe," lived in the woods behind the big house and shared family time evenings on the screened side porch. These were almost the only African Americans the boys experienced in a segregated 1930s Pickens that was a microcosm of the Jim Crow South.

In the meantime, Frances was listening to German language records to teach her (without much success) the language of the country she and the children were to visit. Her knowledge of her German in-laws and of what was occurring in Germany was largely communicated by her mother-in-law Katharina's letter to Charles (Karl), written from Heidelberg and dated January 15, 1935. Translated, the letter read in part:

Dear Karl!

At the long last you allowed me once again to receive some news from you after I have been in anxiety about you for so long a time; after all, it was not nice of you simply to forget your mother when she had become, again, grandmother. But now I am very happy about it and am only saddened that I am not able to see the two boys; why, after all, are you so far away?… Had I believed that your departure then was to be a parting forever, I believe I would have died, but at the time it was stated, confidently, "in two years I am back again, etc."

The letter continued with her hope for approval of the referendum that day on the Saarland returning to Germany: "May God give that it passes without incident and that the poor, tormented people are returned to their homeland." She scolded her son for his criticism of Hitler:

> Dear Karl, you all are being informed downright falsely; here in our country everything is in excellent condition, nowhere is there any unrest… Throughout the entire war [World War I] foreign nations have not been as venomous against us as they are now, and that entirely without reason, for nobody in the whole world can show a government as we have it, because our government does not serve money or glory but only the people. Has there ever been a ruler who gave up entirely his claim to his salary for the benefit of the people? Our leader ["unser Führer"] lives in the most austere way imaginable and supports himself solely from his writings. His salary, which after all he must receive, is being transferred immediately to the benefit of the widows and orphans of the world war, month after month. Just wait for one more year and see what has become of Germany…

After she demonstrated how thoroughly the Nazi propaganda machine was indoctrinating the common German population, Frau Heuss instructed her recently naturalized American son, "Be proud that your parents and your brothers and sister are Germans. That you, my dear, are an American by now was to be expected, for you could not have acted otherwise considering your position and family, but your German blood cannot be denied when the moment comes, your mother knows that."

As adults, Charles and Richard would hear their mother express how much better their lives would have been if their blood father had lived. This chilling letter, which goes on to tell how three sons and a son-in-law had already been conscripted into the Wehrmacht and another was awaiting his call, later made Charles and Richard wonder how a German immigrant with one brother working for the German war machine and three others and a brother-in-law in the Wehrmacht might have been treated and reacted to during World War II.

Nonetheless, it must have been comforting to Frances to believe that she was taking the children to a country where "everything is in perfect condition, nowhere is there any unrest."

On September 7, 1935, Frances, Charles (aged almost four), and Richard (aged ten months) set sail for Germany on the SS Berlin, bound for Bremen. They had been driven to New York City by Parris Sizemore, Pickens's own African American taxi driver who later played a role in Charles Haldeman's novel *The Sun's Attendant.* Parris drove a private automobile that was loaded aboard the ship. One wonders about where he slept during the two-day drive to New York before his trip home by rail.

Frances and the boys were met in Bremen by the boys' youngest uncle, Kurt, the only brother not yet called to military or armaments service. Kurt took the train to Bremen, expecting to bring Frances and the children back to Heidelberg by rail. Almost sixty years later, Kurt expressed to Richard his alarm when he saw "a large American auto" being unloaded from the ship to be driven back to Heidelberg. "I barely knew how to drive," he told Richard, "and I had to drive more than five hundred kilometers with a mother who knew almost no German and two children, one in diapers."

That automobile was to provide the Heuss family "many beautiful tours" during the following six months. Frances fell in love with the family, especially her mother-in-law, Katharina Heuss, and her sister-in-law, Erna Feuerstacke. During their six months in Germany, little Charles attended four-year-old kindergarten, the Heuss family took many trips in Frances's automobile, and little Richard (Dicky) learned to walk. At age four and a half, little Charles returned to the USA speaking German. Unfortunately, a scrapbook kept by Frances of the trip during a critical part of the Hitler years in Germany has been lost. It revealed that Frances actually saw Hitler during her time in Germany.

Postwar correspondence between Charles and his German grandmother tells more about the 1935–36 trip. In 1947 Charles sent his Oma a care package, followed in 1948 by a letter and picture, which she showed to his German uncles. She replied to "dear Charlie and dear Dicky," telling Charles, "I take from it that you enjoy learning and want to become eventually someone great. That makes me feel glad for your father who died so early, and who, too, was an achiever and who no doubt is happy to see his dear sons endeavor to learn. Do you, dear Dicky, like to learn, too? It is a pity that you cannot remember anything of your life here. You were so small, had your first birthday here, year old, and learned to walk here. Can you still remember me, or perhaps 'Kinni,' dear Charles?…The girl liked you a lot, especially you, dear Dicky… She has a boy of five years, her husband was killed in the war and she has been married again and lives in Berlin…

"Dear Charlie, I gladly believe you that you want to come to Germany some time, and I would be very happy if I would still be alive then. For it will take several more years yet before Germany will be beautiful and strong again and we have at least enough to eat. [Oma died in 1952, three years before Charles was able to return to Germany.] I remember with joy the time when you and your mother were here and we took beautiful automobile tours. The kindergarten teacher whom you mentioned in your letter I have not yet seen or met. I shall visit her some time. What do you want to become eventually, my dear?"

Frau Heuss concluded with news about Charles's cousin Gretel, Erna's daughter, who was later to inform Charles of their oma's death in 1952 and whose family was Charles's first host when he came to Germany in 1955. In 1961, when Frances returned to Germany with her second husband (employed by the Air Force Base Exchange in Bitburg), she renewed her close friendship with Erna as well as other living members of the Heuss family. She was finally able to relive the 1930s memories she had kept secret for decades from all but her two older sons.

## III

# A New Father, a Tragic Loss, a New Home

Following the return from Germany in 1936, Frances realized the need to earn her own way if she were to support her two boys. She applied to a hotel management school in Washington, DC; was accepted; and moved to Washington, leaving her sons in the care of their grandparents, Frank and Pearl McFall, in Pickens. Charlie was already a precocious boy with school experience in a German kindergarten. Dicky was growing into boyhood. Both boys particularly loved their grandfather Frank and often competed for his attention, as when Charlie nursed a wounded bird and Dicky, in turn, begged his grandfather for a bird, which he received and accidentally squeezed to death. Both their grandfather and their uncle Waddy, with his wonderful backyard shed and cowboy records, spent hours with the boys.

In Washington, Frances met and fell in love with a fellow student, Willard "Bill" Haldeman. He had been born in Staunton, Virginia, his mother's home, but reared in Youngstown, Ohio. After graduating from Shepherd College in West Virginia, then a two-year school, he held a number of jobs during the Depression before obtaining a basketball scholarship at Stetson University in DeLand, Florida, and earning a degree in business in 1933. At Stetson, Bill was known as Buddy, and he was a fun-loving student featured throughout the 1933 yearbook. After graduation, however, he found difficulty in finding employment as a bookkeeper, for which he was trained, and he lacked the education to become an athletic coach, his real dream. His model was high school classmate Wes Fesler, star football player at Ohio State and later coach at Ohio State and Minnesota.

Though Bill Haldeman was a year older than Frances, she was much older in life experience. While he was attending college and enjoying an active campus life, she was a wife and mother. By the time she met Bill, she had been widowed with two children and visited Hitler's Germany. She was romantic and introspective, loving to read and to travel and to chronicle her children's lives in journals that, unfortunately, do not survive. Bill Haldeman loved sports and physical activity, but his apparent extrovert nature covered a deep sadness he had felt since losing his mother as a teenager and living with an autocratic father and religious fanatic stepmother. Frances was ambitious; Bill wished only to earn a living and live a comfortable life that included golf and other outdoor activities. In those Depression days, hotel management seemed an opportunity to make a good living.

Despite their differences, Frances and Bill fell in love and were married in 1937. The marriage lasted forty-five years and produced three more sons, bringing to five the number the couple reared. It survived despite continual disagreements and arguments that tore her sons between an ambitious mother wanting to guide their lives and a passive father hesitant to assert himself at home or at work.

Only Charles, who became Bill Haldeman's adopted son, developed a personality rising completely above this conflict. Though he formed a lifelong strong bond with his mother, he resisted her attempts to guide his life, and he set and achieved goals despite obstacles created by family situations. Before he met his new "Daddy Bill," Charles had started first grade and was already reading—and writing. He loved movies, serials, and comic strips and drew his own comic strips while a first grader.

In March 1938, the Heuss boys suffered another tragic loss: Frank McFall died of a stroke. For Charles and Richard, he was not only a grandfather but also their father figure. It was the second such loss for Charles, only six years old. Frances, pregnant with her first child by Bill Haldeman, returned home and gave birth on August 24, 1938, to Willard Haldeman Jr. Charles and Richard joined their mother and new brother that fall in leaving for Washington to be with their new Daddy Bill.

Frances, Bill, and the three boys moved to Mount Rainier, Maryland, a Washington suburb. The boys saw little of their new stepfather, who slept days and worked nights in a Washington hotel. They enjoyed watching Daddy Bill put on his suspenders each afternoon on the way to work. There his duties included carrying a drunken well-known US senator up to bed each night.

Charles began second grade in Mount Rainier, where, as always, he stood out as a student and played a lead role in the school Christmas pageant that his four-year-old brother, Richard, attended.

# IV
## BECOMING A FAMILY: NEW YORK CITY
### ADVENTURES

The following year, 1939, Bill Haldeman received a position in a New York City hotel; and the family moved to Riverside Drive in New York City. Here their family unit also included Grandmother Pearl McFall (Gramma), who was taking a journalism course at Columbia University to advance her writing career, and Uncle Waddy, who had begun work at the American Museum of Natural History.

New York opened a new world for Charles, who entered third grade in the city's public schools in the fall of 1939. Frances purchased dozens of sugar cubes for the igloo he built as a school assignment, and she and Bill used the leftover ones for their coffee.

He and Richard, who entered kindergarten in 1939, enjoyed walks with Frances to the nearby park, where they learned to sled in winter. Sometimes a friend (the family had no car) would take them for a ride through Manhattan, where the boys would try to identify the tallest skyscraper. In 1940, the boys viewed the Macy's Christmas Parade with its huge balloons, including that of Superman, which the boys knew from the popular comic book.

The best description of the Haldeman family's New York City years was written by Charles Haldeman himself in a passage possibly planned for but deleted from his novel *The Snowman*. Though place names are sometimes fictionalized, the description rings true to the time, place, and events of the time as his brother Richard also remembers them.

In part, Charles wrote, "They lived then in Manhattan, on 110th Street between Broadway and Amsterdam Avenue… The boy's mother…was pregnant with his third brother and praying mightily for a girl. His father worked nights in the Babin Arms Hotel and slept till noon. His mother's brother, who stayed with them, took delight in bringing home such choice items as skulls and mummy's ears from the Museum of Natural History, where he was painting backdrop landscapes for wild animal exhibits…

"Just down the street on Amsterdam Avenue the Cathedral of Saint John the Divine was interminably going up; paper boats sailed down the gutters; bottle caps were more highly prized than any marbles but steelies; cleanliness—in the guise of a Chinese laundry—stood next to godliness, a Christian Science temple whose almost windowless face repelled all stickballs.

"Comic books were still sixty-four pages for a dime, except for Nickel Comics, which had thirty-two pages and Bulletman. Dixie Cup lids, when you had licked the ice cream off and removed the protective wax paper, revealed the faces of movie stars, sometimes different from ones you already possessed. Popsicles cost three cents each, milk was frequently still in bottles, and potato chips were all of twenty cents a shopping bagful at the five-and-ten.

"The Hudson stank deliciously, making Riverside a pungent paradise of monkey bars and Good Humor men. The boy skated inexhaustibly and he went through the knees of countless pairs of knickers, kneeling and decorating miles of black pavement with bits of brick and pebbles… He learned to whistle through his front teeth and was warned by a cop on horseback that he'd get buckteeth like his horse if he kept it up. In winter he slid on cartons and barrel tops down the packed hillside just off the Columbia campus, had at least one fight a day and two bloody noses, memorized the Twenty-Third and One Hundredth Psalms, and won a New Testament with his name on it.

"He attended Public School 165, a brick labyrinth in whose distant upper reaches lurked something called 'high school,' more awesome than hell… (He) loved fire drills because they went out to stand on Broadway, and when ladies passed by on their way to the Mah Jong Club, they could make rude noises without being identified…

"His grandmother came up from Carolina… his new brother was born (his mother wept), and his uncle left for Montana on a mountain lion hunting expedition…"

(In his unpublished autobiography, Waddy McFall described this adventure provided by the Museum of Natural History, during which he met many national celebrities.)

Charles's description of the New York City years continued: "They went to the World's Fair, miles on the El, and his grandmother…actually took the parachute jump and accompanied his first brother, who was six at the time, into the papier-mâché 'shoot the chute' shaped to look like a small mountain. But they both got claustrophobia halfway down and abandoned their flying carpet, which came shooting out all by itself, much to the amusement of everyone outside. After an interminable pause…the two delinquents emerged headfirst and on their hands and knees, shedding bitter tears, gasping for air, and followed by a close-packed entourage of screaming infants and apoplectic parents." His brother Richard remembers his role in this childhood trauma.

Charles formed a friendship with a delicatessen owner who provided him free tickets to Palisades Amusement Park and to the movie theater where he was able to view four serials *(Hawk of the Wilderness, The Green Archer, The Lone Ranger, and Zorro)* and win three door prizes: a chicken, an Esterbrook fountain pen, and a year's subscription to *Boys' Life*. Charles described many other adventures. Richard accompanied him to the movies once, to view *The Mummy*—it was another childhood trauma.

Bill Haldeman worked part-time at the New York World's Fair in addition to his hotel position and planned to take courses at Columbia University in physical education to prepare for a coaching career. As war began in Europe and approached in the United States, these plans were placed on hold. When the family emerged from a subway in June 1940 following a trip to the World's Fair, the newsboy was calling out news of the fall of France.

The family grew again on January 16, 1941, with the birth of a fourth son, James (Jim). When the baby was brought home, Charles was rebuffed by "Gramma" Pearl McFall in his attempt to go in and see his mother. For Charles, so often separated from his mother, this was unforgivable. It created a distance between him and his grandmother that lasted the remainder of their lives. Despite this incident, the New York City years had bound Bill, Frances, and their now-four boys into one family.

# V

# THE NORTH COUNTRY: AN IDYLLIC SUMMER BEFORE THE WAR

The military draft began in 1941, and though Bill Haldeman had a high draft number due to his age (thirty-two) and size of his family, he felt an obligation to, and saw an opportunity in, the growing military buildup. Shortly after Jim's birth, he left hotel work to accept a warehouse position with the Post Exchange at Pine Camp (now Fort Drum) near Watertown in Upstate New York's North Country.

Frances and the boys moved back to Pickens for the remainder of the 1940–41 school year before rejoining Bill for an idyllic 1941 summer in a cabin at Lake Bonaparte in the Adirondacks. In his unpublished description of the 1939–41 years, Charles described the summer of 1941:

> That summer the boy learned to swim, both on and under water, to tie simple flies, start up an outboard motor. He trapped tiny crayfish with his hands, fished for bullheads and bass and sunfish with a bamboo pole, and cleaned what he caught himself (though his mother cooked it). He rowed almost daily across the narrow end of the lake, by swamps of cattails, to…(the) General Store, which had a wood-floored skating rink downstairs and catered to the needs of summer inhabitants, weekend tourists, and mobs of Boy Scouts from… just down the shore.

Charles and Richard spent hours at play, in and out of the water. Charles cut a limb and fashioned it into a bow to act out scenes from *Hawk of the Wilderness.* Richard caught crayfish, learning to breathe underwater without realizing it. He provided these to fishermen, especially the boys' friend Fred, a widower, and his two old maid sisters from Syracuse. Frances made friends, as she always easily did, and rowed across the lake to shop at the little store there. Bill's work and travel time kept him absent much of the time, except on weekends, as he adapted to his new work with the military.

That fall the family relocated to Carthage, New York, near Bill's work, where Charles began fifth grade and Richard, second grade. Charles was already distinguishing himself at school, filling notebooks with comic strips featuring his own superheroes and writing an essay on the Soviet-German Pact that showed a precocious knowledge of foreign affairs for a ten-year-old. He loved the *Quiz Kids* radio show and pictured himself as a quiz kid as he competed with the children on the radio to answer the show's questions. Both boys spent hours at the local movie theater, watching *Superman* serials and Gene Autry movies, but Charles was ready to move to heavier fare and particularly liked the film *How Green Was My Valley*.

During these months in Carthage, Bill Haldeman adopted Charles and Richard, who became Charles Heuss Haldeman and Richard Heuss Haldeman, sharing the surname of their younger brothers.

America entered World War II in December 1941. Charles heard on the radio of the Japanese bombing of Pearl Harbor December 7, and Richard learned of it in the feverish conversation of the children with whom they walked to school the next day, Monday, December 8. The war was to cast a pall over that Christmas and be all-consuming in the months that followed. It brought a new seriousness to Pine Camp and Bill Haldeman's work there.

# VII

# SACKETS HARBOR: A HOME FOR THE DURATION

Unknown to the boys, their parents purchased a deserted home in Sackets Harbor, a historic village on Lake Ontario, and hired two carpenters to restore and expand it for their family. While the house was being prepared, they moved temporarily to a farm near town, an experience Charles fictionalized in his second novel, *The Snowman*. In May 1942, the family moved to the home in Sackets Harbor it would occupy for the next five years—Charles's only home for that long until he settled in Greece in 1957. By the time he finished the fifth grade in Sackets Harbor, he had already moved eight times and attended schools in the nation's largest city; a suburb of Washington, DC; and three small villages located in three states.

Richard was not so fortunate. After missing much of the second grade in Carthage with almost the entire list of childhood diseases, he was withdrawn from school and started the second grade again in the fall of 1942. Although Bill Haldeman had to drive twenty-five miles to Pine Camp each day in the family's 1938 Ford, Sackets Harbor provided the family a stable home where the children could learn and grow. Although Sackets Harbor is Charles Haldeman's model for the fictional town of Joseph's Landing in *The Snowman,* it is more accurately described by Richard Haldeman in his unpublished short story "Hero's Son":

> Sackets Harbor is a small town. It is not an ordinary small town; located near the northern tip of Lake Ontario in New York State, it was once a proud army town, the defender of America's northern frontier in the War of 1812. It became almost a ghost town after World War II before being reborn in

the 1980s as a tourist attraction and a bedroom community for Fort Drum and the affluent St. Lawrence towns to the north.

Those of us who lived there seventy-five years ago knew a different Sackets Harbor. The Sackets Harbor we knew then was a result and a part of the Second World War. More than that, it was a casualty of the war… for more than 130 years, Madison Barracks was Sackets Harbor. Madison Barracks was more than an army camp to the town; it was her backbone and symbol. It had trained soldiers since the War of 1812, and the famed soldier-explorer Zebulon Pike was buried in the town's military cemetery after losing his life in that war. Ulysses Grant served at Madison Barracks as a young officer, and General Mark Clark was born there. Memorial Day was a special holiday in Sackets Harbor during the Second World War. Led by an honor guard from Madison Barracks, the children of the school, each carrying flags and flowers, would march to the cemetery beyond the barracks, where they would lay flowers on the graves of heroes of many wars.

What this description omits are winters of two-and three-foot-deep lake-effect snows and below-zero Fahrenheit temperatures that lasted from Thanksgiving (or before) until Easter (or later). Southern-born and bred Frances often had to melt snow on her gas oven to provide water. Bill rose before dawn and often had to follow the snowplow to his work at Pine Camp. Still, years later, Frances remembered the Sackets Harbor years as the happiest of her life. The Sackets Harbor home was the last one she and Bill would own until their retirement.

That home, with a bedroom for the parents, a room for Charles, and beds in the attic for the other boys, was located across the street from Madison Barracks and the adjacent town park. A high barbed-wire fence surrounded the barracks and separated town boys playing football, baseball, and war in the park from the Italian and German soldiers imprisoned at the barracks as the war progressed.

Charles thrived in the small town, becoming the star student of its small school and making numerous friends. Though his novel *The Snowman* later belittled the Boy Scouts and the church youth fellowship, Charles was active in both. He loved to swim, and the family traveled one summer to his Boy Scout Camp in the Adirondacks to watch him earn swimming and lifesaving merit badges.

Like the chief character in *The Snowman,* he took over the Sackets Harbor paper route for the closest daily paper *(The Watertown Daily Times).* He built the route to such a large circulation that when his brother Richard succeeded him, Richard had to divide the route with another boy. Charles took money earned from the route to purchase a thoroughbred collie, the breed popularized by the *Lassie Come Home* film. He was chosen to deliver Lincoln's Gettysburg Address at the town Memorial Day. Through his weekly collecting duties for *The Watertown Daily Times,* Charles became acquainted with virtually everyone in town, providing him material he later used in his novel *The Snowman.*

Charles soon outgrew the books Frances read to Richard, such as *Hans Brinker, Little Men,* and *Tom Sawyer,* moving to Lincoln biographies, Sinclair Lewis's *Main Street,* and the current best sellers at the town library, located in the local Presbyterian church. He read the monthly issues of the *Reader's Digest* from cover to cover. He became obsessed with the war and followed its progress in the newspaper and on the radio by placing multicolored tacks of troop positions on a world map kept in his room. The war was also brought close to Charles by his learning that it had claimed relatives of his school's principal, Mr. Huttemann, a Filipino immigrant, and by his viewing of home movies of the attack on Pearl Harbor made by the MacAnulty family who had moved from Hawaii.

He began his own book collection, with each book containing the inscription "From the Library of Charles Haldeman." Yet he also loved and participated in athletics, becoming a good swimmer, playing tennis and softball, and shooting hoops in the backyard with Dad (Bill Haldeman). In the tenth grade, he went out for football (which he later played for a year at Pickens High School), and his best friend was an athlete who moved to nearby Black River and became a star there.

After the war, in the spring of 1946, at only fourteen years old, Charles wrote a variety show in which most of the town's children performed. His careful listening to radio shows of the time enabled him to interject humorous skits and jokes between talent acts. The show was performed twice before large local crowds.

At home Charles lived increasingly to himself as age and intellect separated him from his brothers and his parents. His mother attempted to understand him, the Charlie who had replaced her lost Charlie, realizing his individuality and special gifts. At the same time, the chasm grew between him and his dad, Bill Haldeman. Richard remembers it erupting one time into physical punishment of Charles, though not nearly as violent as the scene later depicted between father and son in Charles's novel *The Snowman.*

In May 1943, Frances Haldeman had given birth to her fifth and final son, Neil, finally accepting that she was never to bear a daughter. Neil was delivered at home by Dr. Sammy Marritt, the town doctor. Dr. Marritt and his wife, Ruth, were the Haldemans' best friends. The town's only Jewish family also included three children—Ann, Manny, and Naomi—whose ages matched up roughly with Willard Jr., Jim, and Neil Haldeman. Dr. Marritt is loosely a model for a character in The Snowman. In the 1950s, when the Marritts had moved to New York City, they were gracious hosts to Charles there during and just after his time in the Navy.

Although the size of the Haldeman family was unusual for the war years, it was by no means as large as Charles sometimes gave his friends to believe or that events in *The Snowman* indicate. Each brother's birth distanced Charles farther from the mother whose attention he longed to keep for himself. He could not blame them, but he could resent his grandmother for depriving him of seeing his mother after Jim was born. After all, his mother was all he had when he lost his father and grandfather. They shared a relationship no one could block or trespass.

Bill Haldeman's colleague in Post Exchange work, Florence Louth, played a special role in the family's Sackets Harbor years. Unmarried and dedicated to taking care of her widowed mother, who had been a prominent Watertown businesswoman, Florence was a large robust outgoing woman who one Christmas played Santa Claus to the Haldeman boys. In the postwar years, she became an aide to and confidante of Governor Nelson Rockefeller of New York, enduring the breakup of his marriage and affair with the woman who was to become his new wife and consoling him through the loss of his son. Florence and her mother had a special friendship with Charles. Her five-page handwritten letter to Bill Haldeman following Charles's death describes this friendship and the Charles of the Haldemans' Sackets Harbor years:

> "Charlie was not a run of the mill sort of guy. My Mother was captivated by him, & that itself was something. She also treated him as an adult & not as a growing boy—but that was old Charlie—he used to sit under our pear tree in the backyard & draw comic strip characters…as she busied herself getting a picnic lunch for the two of them to consume as they sat and yacked away… Charlie always was old for his years, he was smarter than the devil in school, he was a history buff at a young & tender age, remember his speech at the old military cemetery in Sackets Harbor? Was he twelve then?…There also was the time he conducted a prayer service because the minister for one reason or another was not available. No, Bill, your son Charles was different."

Before leaving Sackets Harbor, Charles and Bill had six months to bond there as father and son. Frances had moved to Pickens with the other sons in January 1947 to be with her sister Rosa, who died that year of cancer. Bill remained to sell the house and for Charles to complete the tenth grade. Bill had also to sell the doughnut shop he had opened in Sackets Harbor after his Post Exchange job expired at the end of World War II. Business at the shop became slow after Madison Barracks was closed, and Frances mainly ran the shop while Bill took a job with the welfare department.

In June 1947, Bill and Charles Haldeman arrived in Pickens to reunite the family. Charles was fifteen; Richard, twelve; Willard Jr., eight; Jim, six; and Neil, four.

# VIII

# A South Carolina Sojourn, Move to Paradise, Paradise Lost

Although the McFall family home in Pickens was large, the arrival of seven Haldemans in 1947 challenged its capacity. Already there were Gramma (Pearl McFall) and Waddy McFall and his family. Uncle Waddy had served five years in the Army and was now married with one son and another on the way.

Altogether, eleven people—five adults and six children, representing three generations—would be living there. It was imperative that Frances and Bill find new housing soon.

Following Frank McFall's death, Pearl McFall had attempted (unsuccessfully) to raise chickens. Now she was experiencing some success in buying and selling antiques and had visited the Haldemans in Sackets Harbor on one of her trips. Waddy was working for the wildlife department. Before the war, he had left the American Museum of Natural History to move to Montana. His short time in Montana before entering the Army left him with a desire to return there, which was fulfilled several years later. He had married Pickens County–native Evelyn Roper during the war. He was soon to be elected game warden of Pickens County.

Charles and Richard explored the many treasures of the McFall home, which included a full collection of *National Geographic* magazines dating to the early twentieth century and a trove of novels and histories, including *Gone with the Wind* and *Red Hills and Cotton,* written by Pickens County– native Ben Robertson, friend and colleague of Edward R. Murrow. Charles particularly enjoyed the adventure stories of Richard Halliburton. In the evenings, the family gathered for talks on the screened side porch while the children chased fireflies outside. At the bottom of the hill leading up to the McFall home lived the Singletons, another family with five boys. The basketball court on their lawn attracted the town's children to their home.

Difficult as it was to leave the McFall home, the Haldemans were able to find another well-located house. Bill and Frances rented a roomy home on Main Street, with a side porch perfect for the Bendix washing machines that Bill purchased to start a laundry. Though the self-service laundry pretty much required twenty-four hour monitoring, the business boomed. The home was near downtown, with its movie theater and the Presbyterian church the Haldemans joined.

Though the boys' great-grandmother had died, the remainder of the family's large contingent of relatives was still there, including several cousins of the boys' ages. Charles made many friends, excelled in the classroom, and played on the football team. His knowledge of history and breadth of reading exceeded that of his classmates and many of his teachers. South Carolina, in 1948, was only just adding a twelfth grade; and it was clear that Charles would be one of those chosen to go straight to college from the eleventh grade.

In the fall of 1948, Charles entered Erskine College, a Presbyterian college in Due West, South Carolina, at which his grandfather's first cousin, Dr. J. Mauldin Lesesne, was history professor and future president. Though Charles had not yet reached his seventeenth birthday when he entered, he excelled in the classroom and made special friends with the contingent of Italian American students from New Jersey, who nicknamed him "the artist" for his ability to draw. Several of the Jersey boys were on the basketball team, which Charles enjoyed watching as it earned a small college national tournament berth.

Bill Haldeman's dream was always to return to Florida where he had enjoyed his college years at Stetson. The great success of the laundry enabled him and Frances to put money aside to purchase a business that would be less time-consuming and enable the family to move to Florida. During Charles's year at Erskine, the Haldemans subscribed to Florida newspapers and learned of and then purchased a "personal service center" in a Sarasota upscale motel complex, Florasota Gardens. The final week of March 1949 the family, minus college student Charles, moved to Sarasota, Florida. It rented a gulf-front cabin on Siesta Key, still a quiet dirt-road community bordering miles of beautiful undisturbed beach, and assumed operation of the personal service center.

Charles, meantime, was developing progressive ideas, distancing him from the segregated South and Erskine College. He discovered in Antioch College in Yellow Springs, Ohio, a college fitting his more liberal views and asked to transfer there. Frances and Bill complied with his request, and he was accepted at Antioch for his sophomore year. With a year of college behind him, Charles joined the family in late May of 1949 for a summer of happiness playing in the Gulf of Mexico on the Florida west coast.

Charles, his parents, and Richard were also delighted that the Whitis family from Massachusetts had moved next to them with their five boys with ages almost equivalent to the Haldeman sons. Though younger than Charles and still in high school, the brilliant oldest son, Peter, shared Charles's growing interest in social justice, becoming Charles's intellectual companion as well as friend. Later, as a student at Berea College in Kentucky and as a psychiatrist, Peter was to become a leader in bringing about racial justice during America's civil rights struggle. The Whitis's second son, Bobby, became Richard's friend and remained so even after his family moved to Tampa.

Sarasota itself was winter home of the Ringling Brothers and Barnum & Bailey Circus and spring training site for the Boston Red Sox baseball team featuring future Baseball Hall of Fame players Ted Williams and Bobby Doerr. This provided wonderful opportunities for the Haldeman boys. Frances and the younger boys signed up as extras for the Cecil B. DeMille film *The Greatest Show on Earth* that was to be filmed there in 1950 and 1951. Richard attended Sarasota High School, across the street from Florasota Gardens and within walking distance of Payne Park where the Red Sox played. Once he passed on the sidewalk Cornel Wilde (whom he identified) and other members of *The Greatest Show on Earth* cast. (Later, all the Haldeman boys except Charles, already in the Navy, were able to watch the parade scene for the movie being filmed.) At their business, Bill and Frances met other famous people such as Olympic and golf athlete Babe Didrickson Zaharias and her husband, wrestler George Zaharias. It seemed the Haldeman family had found its paradise.

Bill and Frances were soon to discover, however, that the 1940s Florida tourist season lasted only from Christmas to Easter. Business at their personal service center—including barber and beauty shops, honey and fruit sales, and babysitting service—fell off drastically the very month they moved to Florida. By the late summer of 1949, they were forced to move twice to ever-cheaper housing, settling finally at Maine Colony, a small residential community five miles from Sarasota. They moved into a cabin in the middle of an orange grove, the cheapest housing they could find. To supplement their income and pay their bills (which included Charles's tuition at Antioch), Bill Haldeman took a hotel management position in Sarasota while Frances Haldeman managed the business.

The boys saw their mother only early in the morning and at night. Frances got them ready for the school bus before leaving for work and relieved Bill after the boys returned home by school bus. Bill would cook a can of beans or make sandwiches for the boys before he left for his night job. Fortunately, after a few months, Bill was able to land a better-paying position as bookkeeper for a Sarasota land developer. He formed a close friendship with his colleague there, Ross Boyer, who was later Sarasota County sheriff. Frances was able to return to housekeeping when the business was sold at a large loss, plaguing the family with debt for years to come.

Despite his parents' problems, Richard remembers this as a happy time. He had a close circle of friends in their little community, including three boys his age and the daughter of the nearby country storeowner. A nearby family, the Clevelands, had sons both his and Charlie's ages. Best of all for the teenaged Richard, Maine Colony was within walking distance of still undeveloped Crescent Beach, which offered him happy days swimming and bodysurfing on the gulf.

As a sophomore at Antioch, Charles was absent from the family during these trying times in the fall of 1949. Antioch operated in a system in which students spent one-third of their time working in a cooperative program off campus. Under this program, Charles was serving as a tutor in Philadelphia during the spring of 1950. As the end of the tourist season drew near that spring, Bill and Frances realized they could no longer afford his tuition.

In April 1950, Charles Haldeman was forced to withdraw from college. Though he was still only eighteen years old, his childhood was over and he was soon to be on his own the remainder of his life. Frances Haldeman never lost her guilt for Charles's withdrawal from college. (She attempted to atone for it many years later by providing financial support while he wrote *The Sun's Attendant*.) Charles sought a job in Sarasota, almost impossible to find in the off-season. He finally located one setting pins in a bowling alley. This was hazardous duty as bowlers often bowled the heavy ball before he had finished resetting the pins. He did earn money, however, to enroll for classes at Ringling School of Art, where he developed his drawing skills.

Charles also continued to be a prolific reader, especially enjoying such satiric and political novels as George Orwell's 1984, Sinclair Lewis's *Babbitt, Main Street, Arrowsmith,* and *Kingsblood Royal,* and Philip Wylie's *Generation of Vipers* and *When Worlds Collide*. He took delight in teasing his mother for being guilty of *momism,* Wylie's term for possessive mothers. These "moms" had been criticized during and after World War II for producing weak American men. Afterward, in his letters to his mother, Charles expressed the difficulty he felt in separating himself from her and expressing his own individuality. He also sometimes criticized his friends— not always American—for this same perceived weakness.

In June 1950 the Korean War began, and young men were again being called into the military. To avoid the bloody infantry war that ensued and to relieve financial problems at home, Charles enlisted in the Navy. In October he left for San Diego for boot camp, leaving the Haldeman family unit. In early 1951, Bill Haldeman reentered Post Exchange work at Fort Benning in Columbus, Georgia, where his family rejoined him in March. Bill's dream of a Florida paradise had long since proved a mirage; this chapter in the family odyssey had come to a close, but Charles Haldeman was embarking on a new journey—alone.

# PART TWO

# The San Diego Years, Sailor Ashore 1950–53

# I
# California, Here I Come: San Diego, 1950–53

Charles Haldeman was to make only a few brief visits home over the remainder of his life. When he left for the Navy in 1950, the separation from family was to be permanent for him, as it had been for his German-American father. The ocean that separated Charles Heuss from his mother and brothers at the time of his death was to do the same for his son, Charles Haldeman. From 1950 on, Charles Haldeman was known to his family largely through his letters home to "Mom and Dad," Frances and Bill Haldeman. From this point on, Charles's life as a man and an author was revealed to his family mainly through these letters, other correspondence, and his novels, published and unpublished.

Though Charles had lived as a child in New York City and as a teenage college student in Philadelphia and in towns in the North, South, and Mid-America, the trip to San Diego for Navy boot camp was his first opportunity to view the vastness of America. After traveling to Chicago, he was loaded with thirty-one other recruits into a Pullman car that carried him through the Southwest (Oklahoma, New Mexico, Texas, etc.). He wrote that "The most interesting thing to me was the land in New Mexico which was perfectly flat that it is hard to conceive until you see it. It is like a khaki colored billiard table, or a green ocean, without grass, tree, house or mound, nothing, in all directions, but the horizon."

A few weeks later, he apologized for not writing, explaining to his family, "Everything for the first few weeks is very exhausting with no recreation at all. You get up at 5:00 AM and get to bed about 12 MID., and you have no free time in between—no time for writing letters or mailing them.

"The only thing redeeming about it is the food. You never saw such quantities or variety—for instance on Sunday we had a whole broiled chicken apiece, pea soup, asparagus, lima beans, tossed salad, mashed sweet potatoes, 10 oz. of milk, bread, and a large piece of cake…it is hard to eat half of what they give you…"

His early letters from boot camp revealed that he had heard both from Grandmother McFall (Gramma), who helped rear him during his early years in Pickens, and Grandmother Heuss (Oma), who knew him as a four-year-old in Germany. He continued to hold a grudge against his American grandmother, an aspiring writer who later published histories of the South Carolina upstate but denied him access to his mother after she had given birth to one of his brothers years ago. In a letter to his Mom and Dad, he criticized her attempt to publish: "… she has nothing, nothing, nothing to say, and she has no conception of the character or social intercourse of people." Yet, later, in a letter to Gramma, he wrote: "I certainly hope you sell some of your stories. I guess it's pretty hard for anyone to break into the field quickly even the exceptional writers. But if you keep at it, I don't see why you shouldn't."

He told of a letter he received from Grandmother Heuss in January 1951: "I received a letter from Oma, yesterday. She was very profuse (*auf deutsch*, of course) in saying that they had received the package on Christmas Eve, which I thought was ungodly timing on somebody's part. I'll answer as soon as possible…"

In his same letter to his parents, Charles, now in personnelman's school, had some good news: "I tied for the highest average this first week with a 96.5 average. Every week you are honor man, you receive an extended 48 hr. pass…which spices things up a bit for a class of 33." Charles also revealed he was learning to touch-type—which would be a necessity for his later writing career—and added, "I'm not having any particular trouble with it, being familiar already with a typewriter pretty much…" In a later letter, the son of a Smith-Corona Typewriter accountant wrote, "If I've learned nothing else worthwhile since I've been in the Navy, at least I've learned to touch-type… I am going to buy a nice portable…"

After completing personnelman's school, Charles began to look into the possibilities presented him by Southern California. In June 1951 he wrote, "I am going out to swim in the Pacific for the first time tomorrow. I hope it's a nice day."

The next month he looked forward to visiting Mexico: "The bullfighting season starts next week, so when I get back (from leave) I will be going down to Mexico to see one. It ought to be a real experience…" In a later letter, he described plans to visit the La Jolla Playhouse in San Diego: "Next week I am going to see Joan Bennett and her daughter (Melinda Melarkey I think is her name) in *Susan and God,* playing at the La Jolla Playhouse, which is one of the best of summer playhouses, being entirely professional. It is produced by Dorothy McGuire, Gregory Peck, and Mel Ferrer, and there is always one big name star at least in each performance. They will be putting on plays all through the summer months, and I would like to see as many of them as possible…"

Nine months into his Naval duty, Charles looked forward to visiting Los Angeles, encouraged by the experiences of other sailors in San Diego who had done so. They had visited Hollywood and met actress Billie Burke, who invited them to her radio show and unsuccessfully attempted to help them meet Mickey Rooney. Charles commented, "I just thought it was very nice and certainly unnecessary for her to go to all that trouble, and it goes a long way to show the hospitality of the people in Hollywood; especially it stands out strongly in relief against the shyster attitude of people in San Diego, who are either out to fleece the sailor for all he's got, or steer clear of him as though he had the plague."

When Charles did visit Hollywood, his impressions were anything but positive, as is indicated in a letter describing his visits to Los Angeles in the summer of 1951. He apparently had a (Navy?) friend "Jose" from Los Angeles who brought him access to people there. "I will tell you frankly, the people Jose has introduced me to in Hollywood and Pasadena do not contradict me in this. They are dead movie struck, and they are utterly empty people…"

Charles described several aspiring actors that he met. One, "a TV actress for the Carnation Milk Company," he described as "vacuous, and emotional…now attending a psychiatrist, and encouraging all her friends to do so, too." Another was "a boy who was a Naval flyer in the last war, who came to Hollywood to be an actor…confessedly became a kept man for (Charles named one of Hollywood's top leading men). He was set to marry a girl from his home town when he decided in favor of his favorite male lover, so now he runs an interior decorating establishment on La Cienega Blvd in Hollywood, catering to the stars in more than one way, and living in general a rather useless life.

"The only stimulating and natural people I have met in my trips to Pasadena and Hollywood so far have been some of the adults, and that ratio can't be more than one in five. Three out of the remaining four are alcoholics, and the fourth is just average. If getting away from the base weekends weren't such a boon to my morale, I think I'd stop going up there altogether…"

As his office job in San Diego settled into a routine, Charles expressed his boredom: "I have been doing the same damned job in this place for ten months now, and although you do learn a little bit about everybody's job when you work in one place, still you don't feel that you are quite as fortunate as the person who has made the rounds of a number of various sections and worked in them. I enjoy my job moderately, when we're busy, but right now it's a pain in the neck."

He sought relief from the routine by taking creative writing and painting classes at a college in Pasadena. He expressed to his parents his determination to accomplish something with his time, "In my next letter I want to write you something about the way I feel about some things now, and some of the things I really want to do in the next two years and want to do when I get out, and how I have changed I think since I have been in the Navy…"

In early 1952, Charles sought sea duty to widen his horizon, little realizing that it would be almost two years before this request would be honored. He told Frances and Bill, "My letter of application still hasn't gone into the Bureau, but I keep getting promised that it will, just as soon as a replacement for me can be found. Not that I seemed to be so hard to replace previously."

Meantime he found that living in San Diego had its plus side, telling his mom and dad: "Had a really fine time last Sunday. The boy from New York and I got some pepperoni and bread at an Italian grocery, went out to the park and ate it, then went to see an old French movie with Josephine Baker at a local art theater, out in the sticks. That evening we got a half-pint of bourbon, and a quart of ginger ale, went to the place of a guy who lives off base, and sat talking for some hours. Really there wasn't much activity to the day, but it was certainly one of the most pleasant I have had since I have been out here…

"Mr. Roberts is coming to town, not with Henry Fonda anymore of course, since he is in a new play on Broadway, but with the rest of the cast, and sets, etc. I really want to see it, since I just did miss Henry Fonda in his last performance, in Los Angeles some months ago."

Charles also spent his off-duty time writing and was delighted with his creative writing professor's review of his short story. In February 1952 he wrote, "Yesterday was a good day all around. I took my story to class last night, in its second draft form, and everybody thought it was really excellent. Mrs. Squires, the teacher, said that with a little rewriting to iron out the rough spots in a few places, I ought to have a highly salable property, and that I should submit it as soon as possible. I think I am definitely my own worst critic, and when somebody, or a group of people, are as enthusiastic as those people were last night, it really gives me quite a lift, and no little amount of determination to make something of this interest. Mrs. Squires told me that in all her years of teaching, and writing, she had never met anyone with the natural talent for writing that I have, and she thinks that with an expansion of contact, utilizing experience on a different level from that on which I am now forced to, almost, I should be able to break into print in a quality magazine, such as *The Atlantic,* within a year or so. Of course, this assumes the aspect of somewhat of a pipe dream, unless I dig, and write, and write some more, but last night gave me a boost of a tremendous sort in the direction of wanting to work hard at it."

Visits to Los Angeles were providing Charles to utilize "experience on a different level." In a later February letter home, he exclaimed (in all caps), "The time in Los Angeles couldn't have been more enjoyable; Marian Anderson was superb, tremendous poise and dignity and affability, and a voice which is only hinted at in a recording.

"In addition I ate well and slept well, saw a couple of foreign pictures I had been wanting to see, bought a couple of books I had wanted which are out of print, and visited both the los angeles county museum which is quite an indifferent one, and the huntington library and museum in san marino which has a very comprehensive collection of old manuscripts and some of the first printed Bibles, and many paintings by Gainsborough, Romney, Turer, and Constable…The English of that period that includes *The Blue Boy* and *Portrait of Lady Hamilton* and among a few american paintings, the original one of George Washington that appears on the dollar bill…"

The letter continued with a mixture of praise for Los Angeles's art opportunities and his disdain for it as a city. Charles continued, "Went to the Los Angeles Philharmonic concert here in San Diego last night. They are really quite a fine concert orchestra: especially since L. A. is such a nondescript city really: no one seems to care about anything there except how to seem like one is not."

During the early spring of 1952, Charles and another seaman were selected to escort an admiral's daughter and her friend from the east. Because of a mistake concerning the admiral's name, the training center expected this request might be espionage and put Charles and the other seaman through strict instructions "to remember every place we went, all the furnishings of various rooms, license numbers, etc.…" Charles described the event, "Before the day was over, we were known as 'Undercover Men'…and it was openly believed that we would be found in some ditch Monday morning with our throats slit.

"It soon became clear that Mrs. Thornton had called up for Mrs. Capstaff, and that the Admiral was Capstaff, not Thornton. This the legal office could have found out rather easily I suppose had they not been upstairs watching old Charlie Chan detective movies or something. As it was, we had a very good time, ate a lot, saw the Capstaff's beautiful collie, met the girls who were just seventeen and rather hard to talk to, being quite high-schoolish… Next time, before I become a pseudo-gigolo, I shall ascertain that the girls are in college, anyway, or at least college age."

The monotony of San Diego camp life was finally ending for Charles in the spring of 1952. He was promoted to third-class petty officer and admitted to information school at Fort Slocum, New York. He informed his parents: "I am to be in New York by the 14th of April for the class convening 16 April… I leave here the eighth or ninth… and should arrive the day before Easter in New York. My school is in Fort Slocum, near New Rochelle, about an hour out of Times Square, I think.

"My school lasts for six weeks, starting the sixteenth of April, and lets out on the twenty-eighth of May. I have to report back to San Diego 32 days later… I thought that I would go on to Northern New York straightaway after school [he names people he plans to visit there] and then come to South Carolina for a week or so, or down to Georgia, and then for a little bit to South Carolina, and have time to do everything I wanted to do this summer."

Along with this good news came a disappointment. Charles wrote that he "received a rejection from Harper's on my story…Ah, well. I would have sent it right back out, but I'll be leaving for school before it would return, and wouldn't trust it to be saved or forwarded around this madhouse. I am sending the original MS to you to read therefore, and you can send it on to New York when you finish, to my new address." (Location or existence of this manuscript is now unknown, but it might have been revised to become part of Charles's second novel, *The Snowman*.)

The rejection only increased Charles's determination to write. He described a study plan to prepare him for this career, one that he was to follow in the years to come: "I've been working on a reading list for myself, which will cover a very broad scope, lasting well over a year probably. It will take away the haphazardness of the way I read now, just a novel here and there, interspersed with this or that work of nonfiction. What I am going to read will be broken up into various headings, which begin on a specific level, and expand into broader areas which will be interlocking. It will have its basis in the classics, moving through the classic aesthetic and political philosophers into the writers of the Middle Ages, and from them to the writers whose works have had the greatest effect in crystalizing and focusing the past into the attitudes and civilization of today. All these will be accompanied by their contemporaries in the field of letters, prose and poetry. I have tried to stagger the outline so that I will be able to maintain a picture of the whole thing all the time I am reading, and not get sidetracked on any one theme, to the loss of the whole. I know this all sounds rather presumptive, but I am very much enthused over getting 'started on it,' and if, as Einstein says, 'Education is a love cycle,' then I may make some progress with the whole thing.

"You know as well as anyone that though I have read widely and precociously, I have read with very little purpose, or very little intent toward gaining something definite out of what I was reading. Most of the time in school, I depended far more on cleverness, an ability to put things into words, to abstract, than in actual work, or research. The fact that I made A's and B's means little enough: I deserved F's, because what I have supposedly learned has been a fraud. Sensitivity, and wit, and not a little perception have carried me through everything so far, except the one crucial test of facing up to myself."

Charles bid farewell to adolescence in a letter home in April 1952, expressing how he had changed since leaving home, his understanding of his generation's place in the postwar world, and his plans following Naval service: "You will find, I think, when I come home again, that I have changed an awful lot since the last time I was home, and I don't say that boastfully, since it's about time. I was just thinking: it has been almost exactly two years since I came home that April 17th from Philadelphia [his intern semester at Antioch]. I know how little I had changed really even the last time I was home, from that Charlie who was at the depth of adolescent uncertainty, and general apathy... I have found a little where I am, and a little who I am... The generation that just got through growing up through the Depression, and fighting the last war, was maimed by nothing so much as the philosophy that would not allow them to be either illusioned or disillusioned about anything. The only danger the present generation faces is that it will take what is handed to it, as final and true, and hopeless. We need no cause, we must find our own truth..."

This is a small part of a much larger discourse by a twenty-year-old man already concerned with finding a special place in the world for himself. Charles continued, "The time for me to realize some of my capacity is now, and I think I am going to use my money when I get out to go to Europe for a prolonged stay. In fact, that is the one sure thing I will do when I get out."

**II**

# A New York City Interlude; a Special Family

While attending the information school at Fort Slocum, Charles Haldeman was reunited with the Marritt family, who had been the Haldemans' best friends in Sackets Harbor, New York, during the war years. Dr. Sammy Marritt, who was to be the model for characters both in *The Sun's Attendant* and *The Snowman,* now practiced medicine in New York City. In an April 15, 1952, five-page handwritten letter home, Charles described his visit with Dr. Marritt; his wife, Ruth; and children, Anne (12), Mannie (11), and Naomi (9): "Arrived New York City at 1 p.m. Saturday, took a hotel room near downtown Broadway, got cleaned up and a good night's sleep. Sunday morning I called up the Marritts and was answered by a contingent of junior misses, who got very excited. They gave me directions, or rather Ruth did, on how to get out there, and I took the subway right out there easily enough. I never had such a good time as I did with them over the weekend."

Charles described a busy weekend including a trip to the Ringling Brothers and Barnum & Bailey Circus at Madison Square Garden and a Broadway show, *The River.* (Charles said he had seen Cecil B. DeMille's *Greatest Show on Earth* film earlier "and for the most part it was pretty terrible.")

Charles's family had lived in Sarasota, Florida, and witnessed scenes of this movie being filmed; but Charles commented to his family that he "looked real hard for you, but never could see you."

Charles described the Marritt family: "She (Ruth) and Sammie both look fine, not any older at all. Sammie as rushed and cramped for time to think or eat or anything as usual. The kids are all very big, Anne very sophisticated, Mannie husky, a little taller than (Charles's brother) Jim,

36

I think, and Naomi a little blasé lady, all sass and femininity." Charles was also able to visit with Ruth's mother ("who looks the same") and father ("who has gotten fat and is his same not too pleasant self"). Charles summed up the visit with "They really made me feel like a long-lost brother come home..." Later the Marritts took Charles "to Long Island for a full week, for a sort of cottage party at a country house belonging to Nao's teacher, a voluble Italian woman, and her husband, a screwball hair-dresser—short, fat, loud, and also Italian."

He concluded the letter with a description of the school he would be attending: "There are Army, Air Force, and Marine detachments here, as well as Navy—and all sorts of conveniences and facilities for us, much like Madison Barracks in looks—very old brick buildings, brick sidewalks, etc. [Madison Barracks was the Army base across the street from the Haldemans' home in Sackets Harbor.] Classes start tomorrow. The atmosphere here is far more collegiate than military, so far."

Though there is no evidence he met or taught Charles, Lieutenant Colonel Bruce Hamilton was among the instructors at Fort Slocum in 1952. He was father of Charles's future sister-in-law, Janice Hamilton (Mrs. Richard) Haldeman. Colonel Hamilton died in Korea in 1953. Charles met Janice in spring of 1955 when Richard brought her to lunch at the Haldeman home in Winter Park, Florida.

Upon successful completion of the information school, Charles received the following certificate:

Armed Forces Information School Fort Slocum, New York
*This is to certify that*
Personnel Man Third Class CHARLES H. HALDEMAN, US
Navy Has satisfactorily completed the prescribed course in
Public Information
This 28th Day of May AD 1952

Though Charles had studied at two American high schools and two American colleges and was later to attend Heidelberg University and teach at the Anglo-American School in Athens, Greece, this was to be the only "diploma" he ever received.

# III

# BACK IN SAN DIEGO, TRANSFER DENIED, 1953

Despite his promotion and completion of the information school, Charles was again denied a transfer from San Diego to sea duty. He wrote home in July, "I wasn't disappointed. One cannot express surprise, or disappointment (which is the emotional equivalent of it), in an indulgent way, if one knows that something is going to happen anyway. Being in the Navy, as my friend Roger Long says, is incidental and accidental; in some degree everybody is always in some sort of Navy, or equivalent of it. The important thing to know is that being in the Navy doesn't make you a sailor." This was his first mention of Roger Long, an aspiring artist who was to remain one of Charles's closest Naval friends.

Charles showed his insight into people with his description of a chaplain acquaintance, perhaps a model for a character in his unpublished novel, The Crisscross Row: "I met a young chaplain (through Roger) named Ramberg. He is a very interesting and yet painful sort of person, simply because he is so nowhere. He looks for answers in all sorts of surface things, all objective, never subjective. He has lost his belief in orthodox Christianity, and yet he knows that there is nothing else for which he is prepared. He was in the Navy during the last war as a chaplain also, and then went to Denmark, where his ancestors are originally from, and to Paris and Germany to study. He became interested in Kierkegaard, who is the (or rather was, since he died nearly a hundred years ago) founder of Christian existentialism, the other side of a philosophy which, in its atheistic form, is so popular among the French intellectuals. This interest in existentialism has caused him to lose faith or confidence or something in all the knowledge and belief lying in his background. He literally doesn't know which way to turn."

Charles described Ramberg's wife as "a very intelligent and vital woman, who is about ten years older than he, and who is a half Negro. She had one marriage before which was oppressing her terribly… There is a large element of uncertainty sometimes showing itself still in her personality, and yet she has a tremendous self-control…Ceal (the wife) is able to steady and give confidence to Jay, and he by his very nature is able to inspire self-assurance in her. She has a desire for insight which he only professes to have; he wants package answers, and he won't find any."

In his teens Charles had been confirmed both as an Episcopalian in Sackets Harbor, New York (something he did independently of his family) and as a Presbyterian in Pickens, South Carolina. While he retained his interest in religion, he had become a skeptic; and his experiences with the chaplain (or chaplains) in San Diego made him more so.

On the second anniversary of his enlistment, Charles wrote home with more plans for the future and expression of his philosophy and view of the world:

October 16th—2 years in, 2 to go.

The downhill portion of my enlistment should go extra slowly, if all the days have the same quality of tedium that today has had. Very empty and depleting.

Sent off the letter to Oma [his German grandmother] finally with Dick's [his brother Richard's] picture in it. Must write Gretel [German cousin] also. They are moving soon, I guess.

I plan to take some individual lessons in German here in the next few months, if there is a good tutor here at the San Diego Language School…

Nothing here has any shape, and it is impossible to lend it very much. One introverts, or he spreads out irreparably.

I guess I don't recall ever having met more than eight or ten real people. All of them, I suppose, were anarchists, and quite ready to die, not for something, but as something.

Some of the other people I have known, a very few, maybe had a nice smile, but it was like the wag on the tail of a dog.

This is really a hell of a war [two years into the Korean War].
I forget (no, I don't) sometimes how I got into it in the first
place, and I defy anyone to tell how it makes the least bit of
difference personally, or nationally, or historically, who wins
it—as long as there is anyone fighting it to tell how it makes the
least bit of difference. Personally, I'm not someone who believes
in things no one else does, but perhaps most people just have
short memories stretching to what they believe and know when
they are in contact with the ordinary and the mundane and to
them overpowering workaday world. The world of the real and
vital contains no need for a candid "approach" if we are in it.

Action is candid. Thinking is candid. Real intuition is
candid.

Why hasn't anyone ever fought a war against superficiality
and artificiality? In his birthday suit, of course…

Interestingly, Charles had recently read J. D. Salinger's *Catcher in
the Rye*. profusely praised it, and sent a copy of it home.

A month later, he received news of Oma's death and wrote home:

Today I received a letter from Germany. Inasmuch as it was
edged in black, I knew right away what it would have to say.
Oma died on the tenth of this month after a short illness, and
has been buried in the family burying ground in Heidelberg.
The letter I received was very short. Gretel had written on one
side, and Aunt Erna [Charles Heuss's only sister] on the other.
Erna was concerned that she had not had your address and so
asked me to let you know right away… It was a lot to suppose
that she would live long enough for me to get to Germany and
see her again. In that way two years is a very long time, but at
least she had surely received the letter I wrote her in October.
Perhaps that meant a little something…

The remainder of the letter discusses Charles's progress in learning
German, "rapidly going ahead by far of what German I knew in
college," and his plans to visit a French ship in San Diego harbor with
his friend Roger Long, who was learning French.

In April 1953, Charles learned that his family would be moving from Columbus, Georgia, to Florida, where Bill Haldeman had accepted a Base Exchange position at Pinecastle, later McCoy Air Force Base, near Orlando. Bill left immediately for Florida, and Frances and the three younger brothers followed in June, after Richard's graduation from high school. Richard was to remain for the summer in Columbus, interning as a reporter for the Columbus newspaper and living at the YMCA. Charles wrote that his Navy job had changed, though it was still on base, and he complained about being tied down to Navy work rather than "real things that people I know are participating in; everything that breaks down the walls of this place and makes it into just a part of a big world..."

In a later letter Charles advised Richard on advantages and disadvantages of putting his military service ahead of college. The decision became moot because the Navy was no longer accepting reservists for active duty (Richard had been in the Navy Reserve since January 1953). Fortunately, Frances Haldeman was able to obtain a scholarship for Richard at Rollins College in Winter Park, Florida, where the family had rented a home. A life insurance policy from Richard's birth father, Charles Heuss, paid the remainder of his tuition so he could begin college in September 1953, shortly after the end of the Korean War in July.

Charles was growing impatient with the tedium and "bedlam" of Navy shore duty and longed to be a part of "life on the outside...real things that people I know are participating in; everything that breaks down the walls of this place and makes it into just a part of a big world and not an integrate world of its own, in which every cycle finds its own and isolated life and death and obscenity and sterile glory and a much jaded reality take place. How I long to transfer!"

Charles continued to harbor strong ideas about events in the "outside" world, mired in the Korean and Cold Wars. In June, following the execution of Julius and Ethel Rosenberg, he sent the family a long letter, citing the absence of "mercy" as an "attribute of government." He wrote, "One can only be thankful that there are a few men such as Justice Douglas still around, even though they are rendered impotent by the Clarks and Vinsons. Could anything be so idiotic, for instance, as the statement by Judge Kaufmann in sentencing the Rosenbergs (later echoed by Eisenhower) that 'their crime is responsible for what is happening in Korea' and 'perhaps for a Third World War'? Statements so transparent as those point directly to the guilt and ineptitude of so many people in high offices and their expression in acts of vengeance and half-thinking… All I can even think is that we had better start equating our actions a little more to our professed ideals."

Failure to honor these ideals helped lead to Charles's later separation from his home country. He channeled his dissatisfaction with military life and the actions of the American government through planning his post-Navy life. He wrote to Cambridge University about the possibility of attending there. Meantime, he was busy studying in off hours. He was practicing German with a Thomas Mann reading of chapters from *Tonio Kroeger* and *The Holy Sinner* and pronounced himself ready to "be speaking and reading it like a veteran in a few months. Then Greek." Charles had been entranced by Henry Miller's description of Greece in *The Colossus of Maroussi.* In addition to learning German to study in his father's native Germany, he longed to learn Greek so he could visit or live in Greece. After he moved to Greece in 1957, Charles was to befriend "the colossus" of Miller's book, the writer George Katsimbalis. In 1972 he took Frances and Bill; his brother Richard; and Richard's wife, Janice, to meet Katsimbalis at the Minoan Palace of Phaistos.

A July letter to his parents showed Charles was developing the ability to learn much about a person and a culture in a very short time. He described meeting a Dutch sailor who grew up during World War II in the Dutch East Indies under Japanese occupation. During this time his father was killed and a baby sister died. The young man had been in the US for two years and wished to settle here. Such insightful vignettes were to form important parts of Charles's novels.

In August 1953, Charles finally received the good news he had sought for years: he had been accepted for sea duty. He wrote home, "I will be glad to get out to sea—even though we shan't go much of anywhere until early 1954…I have been horribly depressed a couple of times in the last few weeks. But I know why—it involves primarily the awareness of the absolute gap between applying myself to whatever tasks I have in the Navy for eight hours a day—and then trying at the end of the day to go to the very opposite end of myself—into a world primarily 'mental,' lying in a different universe of values and perceptions and interests and trying to get work, real work, done there… Right now, as much as I hate it, resent it, or see right through it, the Navy is my 'job'—and I am at best a part-part-part-time student."

Charles was to learn that after three years confinement in San Diego, his "job" at sea would open him to new opportunities. It would take him around the world and introduce him to new people, experiences, and insights. These would supplement the "primarily mental…universe of values and perceptions and interests" taking growth within him.

# PART THREE

# The Sailor Sees the World
# 1953–54

I

# PREPARATIONS FOR SEA, LONG BEACH, FALL 1953

Later in August, Charles wrote of moving into a barracks at Long Beach, where he would be stationed until boarding the USS *Stickell* "about the 8th of Sept." The previous week he had trained on another ship, the Rogers, experiencing "motion sickness… not really seasick…" He expressed his delight at his "first opportunity to go on board a ship of the US Navy." The USS *Stickell* was a destroyer, the ships Charles described as "steel platforms where not many years ago (World War II) some people got ground, shredded, dropped, and riddled and melted playing the same games for different stakes. In war, it would not be death that is disgusting—but the fact that each man who dies possesses so little of his own death—as Rilke says." Not yet quite twenty-two years old, Charles showed the preoccupation with death that continued until his indeed premature death. Years later, his close German friend, the sculptor Pieter Sohl, remembered that Charles was frightened that he, like his German father who died at thirty-two, had limited time to discover and attain his purpose in life.

Charles was captivated by Long Beach, with its thousands of sailors and huge shipyard reactivated for the Korean War. He described to his family the crane at the shipyard, "one of the three largest in the world, all the same size, and all built by the Germans. One is at present in Russia, one here, and one sank being towed across the English Channel… It must be over 200 feet high, and it can lift the tremendous weight of 325 tons dead weight… on days such as today, when it is right alongside our ship, it positively towers above anything you could imagine."

Even as he trained to go to sea, Charles continued his preparation as a writer. He sent copies of several poems home "so that if I lose them I'll have something to show." His letters included vignettes of persons

45

he met, including American, French, and Dutch sailors. One described a French-born American sailor and his mother. The sailor "has lived here about 12 years—went back to see his father when he was 17. His mother—who is Russian—is divorced and is now married to Admiral Byrd's right-hand man...whom I did not meet." He described the mother to his mother: "about 5 years older than you, Mom, rather stocky, energetic, nervous, dissatisfied, quite likeable. She is also a wonderful cook; I ate the best leg of lamb ever...when we left she embraced me a la Francais."

Charles's novel *The Sun's Attendant* was later to be filled by such stories of the postwar world. When he arrived at Long Beach in 1953, results of World War II were still present everywhere almost a decade after the war ended: the refugee problem, the rebuilding of Europe through the Marshall Plan, Allied occupation of Germany and Japan, the disintegration of the colonial system, the Cold War, Berlin Airlift, and partition of Germany, the fall of China to communism, the Korean Conflict, which was ended but not resolved by an armistice in July, and the remobilization of the United Nations to fight in Korea.

In 1950, only five years after World War II, members of Charles's generation were called into service in Korea. This generation, now often called "forgotten" or dismissed as "silent," had known little but war and its aftermath. Its members were born in the depths of the Depression, grew up during World War II, and came to adulthood during the Cold War and resultant Korean conflict. Many of their fathers and older brothers, later glorified as the "Greatest Generation," were called back into service and commanded them in Korea.

Lying ahead for Charles was a year at sea that would take him to nations in the Pacific and Asia still bearing the scars of war, always under the danger that his ship would be called to intervene in Indochina, where the French were experiencing defeat. At Long Beach he befriended a French sailor whose "ship will be in France for Christmas, then to Indo-China." As Charles had written many months before, "The only danger the present generation faces is that it will take what is handed to it, as final and true, and hopeless. We need no cause, we must find our own truth..." Though many of his contemporaries did accept what was handed to them, Charles continued to seek his own truth.

In September he was finally able to write home: "Well, our underway training is all over; whew whew, whew…not as bad as all that, but it's a pain having observers all over the ship all the time who do nothing but look for what's wrong. An admiral came on board and said the ship was 'in remarkable condition for a ship in commission so short a time. That made the Captain feel happy and he passed it on…" Almost three years into his time in the Navy, Charles was finally to become a real sailor!

# "Twenty-two...a Strange Age... a Strange Year"

Preparations for going to sea coincided with Charles's twenty-second birthday in September 1953, and he met both with eager anticipation. He wrote his parents, "Twenty-two is going to be a strange age...I can feel it; rather I should say is going to be a strange year."

In his September letters home, Charles described his ship and his place in it. Surprisingly, it contained a television set, something not yet common ashore. Though he had just finished a fourteen-hour day, he described his work as "not exactly dissatisfying; it is not so impersonal as it was at NTC; here I work with many more things, with many more interruptions." His office "which is about 7 by 23 feet" had "a shelf and drawer to keep things in" and he had use of the several typewriters there, making it a good place for him to study and write at night. He said he would "write soon for a few books I want." As personnelman, Charles worked "until eleven or twelve every night... I don't really mind, though. There is much work which must be done..."

Despite his heavy schedule, he planned to use his time aboard ship to advance his own studies. He wrote, "I have decided to concentrate on language almost exclusively the rest of the time I'm in the Navy. I can get no continuous reading done; two or three hours at a stretch is better adapted to study than reading, and I believe it will profit me more." Charles was to become fluent in four languages—English, German, French, and Greek. In a letter he greeted his parents in French and German—"Pere et Mere" and "Mama und Papa."

Surprisingly, despite his German heritage, Charles discovered that "I don't think it will take me anywhere nearly the time to learn French that German has though. I have a much greater affinity for the tongue somehow…" That might be attributed to Charles's friendships with French sailors in San Diego. He wrote of accompanying four French sailors to the San Diego Zoo where, with their limited English and his limited French, "we communicated all five us rather well, and talked about all sorts of everything. Three of them are from smaller Brittany and will be priests… they have studied philosophy and Latin and Greek already. They were pleased because I knew who their popular authors are, and that I had read them, or some of them… If all the French people are like the sailors I have met in SD, I can imagine no more pleasant people existing: naïve, gentle, candid."

Although Charles worked until midnight five nights, he was gratified to "have one night for myself…with a decent place to go after taps" in which to study, something unavailable previously at the naval base. Yet he realized, "It will still be January before I am able to devote significant time to myself, however." In his time to himself, Charles continued his quest to understand himself and his naval experience. He told his parents, "I have felt at times…that I was living in the center of an immense allegory…far from unreality, the consequent very ambiguity of my existence has at times allowed me to transcend personal situation and achieve an imperative insight. Certain finalities… if all were freedom there would be no freedom, just as if all were colored red there would be no red; that is the meaning of the navy. Conformance is not conformance…unless the person is ignorant of there being other choice…or unless he has chosen conformance, but that in itself is an act of freedom…"

Charles's work was being combined with intense training. In October he wrote that the four weeks training he and his shipmates were receiving "is roughly equal to those a half year otherwise" and described an accident at sea in which a boatswain's mate lost a finger and one in which his ship was "caught in the tanker's wash long enough that we grazed her side…not serious but could have been." In another letter he reported: "Out to sea this last week all week day and night… The next five weeks will be hell; we'll be getting trained in battle stations, firing guns, maneuvering, etc.…hard on the yeomen who have to get up every five minutes and go to a battle station which has nothing to do with their normal work." As a personnelman, whose duties are like those of a yeoman, Charles was responsible for all records and correspondence aboard ship.

A month later he wrote his brother Richard of viewing a tragic experience while his destroyer "spent an interminable week at sea chasing a carrier around… The ocean jumped crazily; everybody was sick… One plane was lost over the end of the carrier and sank immediately, pilot inside. A very quick no less permanent for being painless death for him. I think I know quite a bit more than most people about death…in fact I am sure I do, yet I am actually unfamiliar with what it even looks like as a sudden thing. I am not even too sure what sort of a mental context you build up to comprehend there being a death involved…the end of a life…in such an accident as the other day's. Death is so sudden and life is so long, or seems to be and we mistakenly talk and think of them as opposites, when one is the absence of the other really; that is, death is only an idea held by the living."

In another letter, Charles gave Richard, who was taking first-year German at Rollins, a full-page single-spaced "manual" on how to study the language, indicating the meticulous study regimen Charles had set for himself.

Charles also included a copy of Fyodor Dostoevsky's *The Idiot*, recommending it to Richard and Mom as "magnificent." This novel was later to prove instrumental in Charles's thinking and writing.

As 1953 came to a close, Charles's ship returned to receive "services from the pier," and he was elated that "so it will be until January fourth." He had become very ill and lost a great deal of weight during the last week at sea. Back in Long Beach, he received a great deal of mail, including a letter from his friend Roger Long, who "had been to Japan and back already… His ship was sent over to pick up released prisoners of war and bring them back to the states. He is in Philadelphia now."

Roger included in his letter one he had received from a young man he had met in Japan. The letter described in imperfect language but great depth the changes and conditions in Japan in the postwar era. Reading the letter, Charles must have recognized in its author a kindred spirit who was witnessing the same superficiality and lack of direction he was seeing in American life. With its spelling and sentence construction unchanged but with extra paragraphing, the letter read:

17 October 1953

Dear Mr. Roger Long

I received and read your letter with much interest and appreciation and I found that the man like you were rarely seen even in America. And I am very glad to have known you. First of all, let me have my own explanation on the Japanese People's conditions since post-war II. Being set free from the terrible yoke of the militarism, Japan and the Japanese have much changed (as you may be aware of) since post-war. And the Japanese began to started their new life under the name of democracy. But almost of us, I can tell you, could not understand the real meaning of democracy just like the ship without rudder in the sea. And, as a result, there prevailed the individualism (in a ill sense) in every detail of the Japanese.

About eight years have passed since that time. Now the Japanese, of course, really know the true meaning of democracy. Nevertheless we are still wandering, wandering…pretending that we are following democracy in reality. (All patriotism far, far away from the Japanese people's mind, every man is, more or less, low, cunning, except some kinds of people.) In Tokyo, I imagine that you saw a surprising rehabilitation letting you doubt if you were really in Japan. A lot of large building, a constant stream of motor cars, the well-prepared railway traffic, a number of luxuriously dressed women, puny looking lads and the tumultuous musics. When you were walking among these, did you find something wanted in Japan? Did you think that the future of Japan is hopeful? And didn't you feel that everything in Japan is superficial? I think you did.

Here I really know how important a spiritual culture is. With this thought, I admit the important part of literature. So I think I cannot overestimate it too much. (Yes, I take the course of economy, but I must learn about literature and science and etc.…within first two years). In "Democratic Vistas" (One of the texts for English, written by Walt Whitman an American poet) I could find it out.

I had a taste of drawing picture. I told you this before you know Mr. Long. So I am a little more sensitive to the beauty of nature than the other. The view of Japan is especially wonderful in this season at least by my opinion. Deep, clean, blue sky, wonderfully colored mountains dainty air and so on. (I am much fond of rural view.) This is the first experience for me to write to a foreigner, so I suppose you can find out many mistakes (grammatical and with the other reason). Then, please read the part that caused you a hard understanding with some intuition and imagination. (It seem rather impudent to speak such a thing and I should have told you this at the first part of this letter.)

I will waite the next letter from you with a great expectation.

Sincerely yours,
Masatoshi Ikoma

Whether the correspondence continued is unknown, and it is doubtful Charles encountered Roger's Japanese friend when his ship later visited Tokyo. Still it helped make Charles anxious to visit Japan; it increased his liking for the nation when he did so and his desire to perhaps someday live there, one never realized.

Meantime, Charles's store of experiences for future characters in his novels continued to grow. In Long Beach he met a sixty-two-year-old shipyard worker at a downtown doughnut shop and gave a very long description of him in a letter home: "born in Hell's kitchen, brought to France, orphaned, returned to America, raised in a Peekskill, New York orphanage, adopted, ran away, taken in by a priest, and lived in and/or traveled to 'all the states 3 times.'"

Though the events of the man's life grew more and more unbelievable, Charles said, "I told him that I believed him. And I did… Not only did he show through everything he said in a genuine sort of way; everything he said was the farthest thing from bragging… It was a reproduction of himself." Charles's writing made the entire description so vivid that its readers felt they had met this most unusual person.

At the end of the letter, Charles wrote of the death of the poet Dylan Thomas and asked his parents to take $15 from his funds at home to send to a fund to help Thomas's wife and family in Wales. He also sent home a book of Dylan Thomas's poems for his parents to read. In a subsequent letter he asked his mother, "If you get the chance, read the

Dostoyevsky novel I sent Dick [his brother Richard], 'The Idiot.' It is magnificent, really." Richard did read the book, which also became one of his favorites. In it he, like others of Charles's friends, could see similarities between Charles and the novel's protagonist, not an "idiot" but a man whose innocence and Christlike kindness are mistaken for ignorance.

In December 1953, Charles wrote that his ship would be departing "the Twentieth (of January)" for "Japan, Formosa, for three months." During his final days in California, he made a trip into Los Angeles, visiting an exhibit "not very impressive" of Israeli painters; spent two days back in San Diego; shared several political and philosophical ideas with his parents; and sent his parents two poems. He told the family of his plans following his discharge. He would correspond with several schools where might continue his education, including Columbia University, where he might obtain a job and work part-time.

In an introspective letter before leaving for Hawaii, Charles wrote of his continued search for his own identity: "Training is almost over; it is not nearly as bad as I can imagine it might be. If there are things that I'm afraid to face directly, I must know what they are at least. Things that I do, I do too easily… My drawing, my writing: they are facile; I am rarely artless, and if I am, I'm least sure of it myself. That's not the way it should be. I like Roger I think because he is utterly unassuming yet completely 'cognizant.' I still think I do a bit of watching myself from behind my back…and the double vision of it is perverse; it corrupts so many good intentions without disarming them. I feel like the filament glowing in a bulb in a vacated lighted room, and that is not good, not good that I should feel like that about myself."

On January 20, as the USS *Stickell* left port for Hawaii, Charles continued one quest, for self-identity, and began another, for understanding of the people and places of the Eastern postwar world.

III

# DISCOVERING THE WAR-RAVAGED POSTWAR WORLD, 1954

The history of USS *Stickell* while Charles Haldeman was on board (from Wikipedia, the free encyclopedia):

On 2 September 1953, *Stickell* (DDR-888) was recommissioned at Long Beach, Comdr. James Boyd in command. Following training out of Long Beach, she joined DesDiv 21 at San Diego on 18 January 1954. Two days later, she and her division headed for the western Pacific. This deployment consisted primarily of hunter-killer training and Taiwan Strait patrol. On 1 June, she departed Sasebo on a voyage to complete a circumnavigation of the globe. Along the way, she visited Hong Kong, Singapore, Ceylon, Kenya, South Africa, Brazil, and Trinidad, She reached Norfolk, Virginia, on 10 August 1954 and joined DesDiv 262 of the Atlantic Fleet.

Charles described his experiences during and impressions of this voyage in letters home. These letters are to his mom and dad unless otherwise noted. Charles's spelling of Tokyo—*Tokio*—has been altered to the conventional English spelling. Excerpts from the letters follow:

**23 January 1954: En route to Hawaii**

"1500 or so miles out at sea on the way to Hawaii—we arrive Tuesday morning & will be there two days before going on to Japan… I've subscribed to a couple of newspapers—*The Nation* and *The Manchester Guardian*—both weekly—& I'll keep in touch with world news (a couple of weeks late) in that way."

**January 1954: Charles Describes Hawaii**

"It is extremely hot here…looks a little like California, but feels like Miami. The mountains here are beautiful, I suppose, if I could feel them

54

as beautiful." Charles criticized the military atmosphere and said, "I'm glad I'm not stationed here. Tomorrow I'll maybe go to Waikiki…"

## 3 February 1954: Across International Dateline, Visit to Midway

"We lost the first (of the month) crossing the International Date Line, so February this year will be only a 27-day month." Charles discussed Hawaii, "I did go to Waikiki, and it turned out to be quite a nice beach," but was more impressed by Midway, the island that played such an important role in World War II.

"We were on Midway Island this last Sunday for fueling. It has a treacherous entrance, a cut in the coral, quick currents, etc. Exceedingly beautiful natural beach, almost all around the island, with tiny insignificant shells, and pleasing little pieces of coral. All the old fortifications have not been removed; huge pieces of machinery lie rusting in the surf, and half crushed concrete pillboxes sit pinkly under the saw grass at the beach. The island is in a state of disrepute, mostly white wooden military buildings, junk-strewn. No great rebuilding has taken place, and all over walk or lumber birds called gooney birds with huge clapping bills and Ava Gardner eyes. They nest anywhere and chase you if you get too close. I enjoyed this island more than Hawaii somehow."

## Late February 1954 from Yokosuka, Japan, After Visiting Tokyo

"I am beginning to like Tokyo very greatly; in many ways European, and yet the people are not. In general the people have a certain look of intelligence, or acuteness… At any rate, I like these people very much. This week I may meet a girl who is studying at Tokyo University: German and Spanish is what she's studying. She is Japanese and I hear speaks excellent English."

Charles planned to send books home as "Tokyo is a storehouse of books" [Charles discovered books by Henry Miller, banned in the US]; it must have been almost a German city in many ways before the war; the stores are loaded with the contents of old German homes which must have been auctioned or purchased entire." He praised delicious and cheap food he was able to buy in (German and Chinese!) restaurants in Japan.

Charles was delighted that he now had a discharge date of August 16 (two months early). A Navy friend had been discharged and entered Antioch College (where Charles last matriculated) but was alarmed by the "naiveté" of students there, "partly why I [Charles] would never consider going back there now."

## 3 March 1954: Dark Description of Okinawa

"We have visited Okinawa twice—a moody brooding quick tempered island, with turquoise water and South Carolina red clay, patchwork cultivation everywhere. Many Americans died here, and their deaths seem to me to hang over the island, stupidly & depressingly—all this insignificant land—& the white man's crime: land and oppression." The ship was about to depart for a long period at sea, giving Charles the opportunity to study and to save money. He also arranged to send home the books he had purchased.

## 15 March 1954: Experiences and Purchases in Tokyo

"We are still in port, at least until March 17th, the middle of this week." Charles described a trip to Tokyo with a friend from the ship: They "visited a very weird exhibition of modern Japanese painting at the UEANO Park Gallery, mostly surrealistic with nightmarish sexual distortions in bright colors." Later the two accompanied his companion's friend, a divorced woman working in the orthopedic clinic of a Tokyo hospital. The three enjoyed a German restaurant where Charles greatly enjoyed the food and was "still stuffed a day later." Charles described the purchases he made in Tokyo: "a print, woodblock, which is almost as Greek in its fury as Japanese…a dark brown worsted suit, tailored to size by a Hong Kong firm whose representatives were on the ship for several days…for $49, a suit which would cost better than a hundred in the US…and a Longines watch for $36, which retails in the States for $72."

## 21 March 1954: A Letter from a German Cousin

Charles sent home a translation of a letter he received from his German first cousin, Gretel Feuerstacke, daughter of Charles Heuss's only sister, Erna. Gretel, aged eighteen, had asked several questions about immigrating to the US and the opportunities there would be for her there. Charles hoped that Mom (Frances) would be able to help answer these questions. Frances had become a very close friend of Erna during her 1935–36 trip to Germany, and later they resumed a close relationship when Frances lived in Germany from 1961–67. By then, ironically, Gretel had married an American soldier and immigrated to the US, rearing two sons in America. She and her husband still live in New Jersey and Florida.

## 27 March 1954: The "Other Japan"

"We are in Sasebo 450 miles south of Tokyo after a week of general exercises on a gratefully level sea for a change. Scenery is more scenic here, more round pastel; through a good set of glasses colors flash out brightly of a crane, a yellow hangar and hillside Japanese houses. The water through glasses mercurie and knifey, edged with reflected red." Charles said that towns appeared "like forts in a wilderness" yet "88 million people live on these islands, not all of them in cities. I probably won't have the opportunity to see the 'other' Japan." Charles told his parents he has turned down a possible opportunity to remain in the Navy through an "officer procurement program." The executive officer told him "there was no one on board he thought more qualified…I rather wished he had not brought it up, since it places one under that rather vague sense of obligation and sympathy which a statement of confidence or appraisal always does…" He thanked his mother for sending him a *New Yorker* article on Edward R. Murrow, adding, "I certainly hope something comes of his opening barrage against Senator McCarthy." US Senate hearings on the McCarthy-Army conflict were to begin the following month. In early 1954, newspapers, magazines, and radio broadcasts still provided news to most Americans. That year the first Orlando, Florida, television station went on the air, and Charles's family purchased its first TV set and watched the Army-McCarthy hearings.

## April 1954: Kachstung, Formosa, "Chinese and Taiwanese Island"

Charles wrote his parents from Formosa: "This Chinese and Taiwanese Island (they hate each other) is very hot and I hope Chiang is stewing in the juice of it." (Chiang Kai-shek and his Nationalist Army had escaped to Taiwan following Communist takeover of Mainland China.) Charles spoke of the poverty of the island and the promiscuity of the Taiwanese "girls": "The V D rate is near one hundred per cent." He said without "good books" he would go "mad."

"Although I have only four months more, each day is endless…" Charles expressed concern for his friend, Roger Long, apparently suffering from physical and mental problems—"I don't think he is doing any painting at all"—and his delight in receiving a letter from Elizabeth Sale, the novelist he met in Long Beach.

Charles's mother had enclosed in her letter a reply to the letter from his cousin (her niece) Gretel Feuerstacke in Trier, Germany. His mother had apparently suggested that Gretel, who had complained of lack of opportunities in Germany, come to America. Charles questioned that advice and wrote a separate letter to Gretel in which he enclosed his mother's letter. Charles (who was to spend most of his remaining life away from America) wrote Gretel: "We must discover what in our personal and national differences is valuable for all of us, and in what way and how permanently it will be valuable; and conversely what is universal in our concepts of national welfare and the worth of the individual. It is at least our generation's problem as well as it has been others, and if we cannot attack it within the framework of our own societies, despite the restrictions they place upon us, then it will not be done at all..."

## 24 April 1954: Formosa Straits, "Everyone Sweating Indochina"

Two weeks before the French defeat at Dien Bien Phu, Charles wrote home: "It has been almost two weeks since we left Hong Kong, two weeks of sailing in the Formosa Straits...we feel isolated from everything and yet exceedingly vulnerable, as though this world which attacks us, as though our radio is our enemy, the container of the unforeseen...

"Everyone is sweating Indo China. United States policy certainly seems to be indeterminate and frightened not a little in connection with the situation there. We only hope that we will not have to go there, that the conference this month will bring a ceasefire and the hope of valid truce talks...what comes on our radio leaves us feeling very much in an empty vulnerable universe."

The conference Charles spoke of was to begin two days later, April 26, 1954, and continue until July 20, resulting in establishment of the nations of North Vietnam, South Vietnam, Cambodia, and Laos. This conference would not bring lasting peace to Indochina. A decade later, war would erupt there involving all these new states.

## 12 May 1954: Post-Navy Plans, Discharge in Ninety Days

"On our way to Kobe & Sasebo—our last ports before leaving Japan." Charles told of enjoying a picnic in a Japanese park with a journalist friend and watching local life. He asked his mother to secure his birth certificate, name change document, and transcripts of his college courses in preparation for life after his discharge "in 90 days." He had written to Yale for the possibility of entering at midterm and also planned to go to New York and enroll in the fall at Columbia University.

## May 1954: Kobe, a Tragic City, Antagonistic to Americans

After his visit to Kobe, Charles described a city "destroyed sixty per cent during the war... It seems to be more antagonistic toward Americans than any other Japanese city I have been in..."

## 27 May 1954: Indochina Avoided, Heading for Home

Charles wrote home of his relief that the USS *Stickell* was heading for Hong Kong and then for home, despite fears it would be ordered to Indochina. "We will...leave on schedule for Hong Kong the first of June, our final detachment from Japan. I don't think anyone will really feel we are returning to the states until we are past Singapore (about the eighteenth of June) though." He continued discussion of his post-Navy plans: "A letter from Yale: too late for this fall, try us for fall 1955, perhaps. Meanwhile this fall I'm going to enter Columbia University's School of General Studies as a non-matriculated student, and study two courses in German, one in French, one in something else. Then I'd like to go on to Europe next spring as I had planned... Look around thoroughly, visit my friends in four or five countries, relatives in Germany...and come back tentatively in time for the fall term at (possibly) Yale. I should be fluent in German, not too hesitant in French, and can enter as an advanced student, if I apply before I leave for Europe and take all examinations et cetera."

## 31 May 1954: Showing Mother "a Person You Have Never Met"

The closeness of the relationship between Charles and his mother was revealed through his letters home. Although most letters were addressed to Mom and Dad, the correspondence was principally between Charles and his mother. As his ship headed for Hong Kong, Charles wrote two letters illuminating the relationship with her. In one he shared her concern about problems in their South Carolina family encountered by his teenage cousins Carolyn and Frank Cantrell. After death of their mother, Rosa, sister of Frances Haldeman, their father married a woman cold and distant and verbally abusive to Carolyn and Frank. Charles was continuing the "father's" role he had earlier assumed in correspondence with his German cousin Gretel.

In another letter, Charles sought to help his mother understand him through a self-description in a five-page prose poem. The poem began:

> Try something if you can:
> Just imagine that you have never met me before
> That you don't "know me better than I know myself,"
> Or some other such motherly prerogative,
> Conceive, if you will, that as you are reading this letter
> You are coming in contact with a completely different person,
> One you have never met before.

In the four-and-one-half single-spaced pages that followed, Charles strove to describe "who and why and what he is." A key verse reads:

> I am not afraid to die.
> But I find myself unable to die for something
> Until I can die AS something…
> Please inform me if you can
> How a person can die for something
> Until he is capable of dying as something…
> If he is not dying AS something
> He is not dying at all. He is dead already.
> Maybe the horror of this war
> Is that there are so many people
> Who are ready to die for some thing
> Before they are in any way
> Aware that they were ever alive.

In another letter written about the same time, Charles expressed his optimism for the future: "I feel better now than I ever have before in my life. I know that nothing can 'happen' to me which I do not accept or participate in. I am not 'adapted' or 'adjusted.' I am only alive. I can be no more." Awaiting him on the voyage home were more eye-opening experiences, including a visit to Mainland China.

## 9 June 1954: Describing Hong Kong, Unauthorized Trip to China

"We are on our way to Singapore, having left Hong Kong this afternoon." In a long letter, Charles discussed conditions in Hong Kong: "All the British soldiers say that Hong Kong is indefensible, and that if the Reds decided to, they could take it virtually without resistance… Any skirmishes with Communist border patrols are handled by the Hong Kong police, all Chinese, in order to avoid any possibility of an international incident." Hong Kong had swelled from 600,000 to two million residents since the war, Charles said, but "there are no longer droves of political refugees flooding the city." The most interesting part of the letter is Charles's visit to Kowloon with a British soldier friend in the mainland of China, breaking "all kinds of Naval laws by putting on civilian clothing…I had a great time taking part in a collegiate sort of discussion group at the apartment of a Lutheran pastor, a German from Mannheim who has been in China off and on for the last 25 years. Several bright young English servicemen, all very earnest and serious, and one seventeen year old boy who is a student at Hong Kong University, were there."

Charles received an invitation from his British friend to visit his "working class" home in England. Charles realized that despite his friend's intelligence, which would enable him to study at Oxford after his service, he "has suffered in school and elsewhere from the idea of class distinction, something which is pretty foreign to the average American. I think I told you that he will study English at Oxford and will become a teacher."

Charles closed with "one very humorous thing: Mary Soo and her side cleaners." He described how Mary Soo, who owned several rafts and sampans, and her six or seven helpers swabbed down and painted ships in the harbor "in exchange for the ship's garbage (and that's all)…"

## 11 June 1954: Preparing Negro Sailors for South Africa

As the ship approached Singapore, Charles was relieved that they "came as close to Indochina as we will on last Wednesday—two or three hundred miles from Hanoi. A week from today we'll be entering Ceylon." Charles was already thinking ahead to the problems that would face African American sailors when the ship reached South Africa. He told his parents, "In South Africa there will be difficulties for our Negro sailors; they will find segregation of a different, or if not different, an intensified nature." The executive officer of the ship was attempting to prepare the Negro sailors for this, but ironically, "an interesting sidelight of the affair is that the officers of our division of ships have been invited to a big native fete in Durban by the tribal chieftains, and it will doubtless be a wild and splendid and good willed celebration, with everyone getting loaded and stuffed and flattered, and falling head over heels with protocol and comity in the process." Charles discussed in depth the plight of the American Negro, which this indicated: "I think it brings to mind clearly the size of the problem the Negro himself must grapple with (aside from white supremacy and its effects, which are the white man's disease) in American society… that is, his hesitancy and uncertainty concerning his own inherent worth, and his wealth of racial culture. A large portion of his suffering has its inception the moment he begins to become a lesser sort of white man, whether he takes this 'way out' through laziness or ignorance or betrayal outright."

## 26 June 1954: Enjoyable Visit to Ceylon (Sri Lanka)

In a two-page single-spaced typewritten letter, Charles described a visit to Ceylon (now Sri Lanka) where "I made all kinds of friends," including a Muslim businessman who tried to convert him to Islam, sell him jewelry, and go into business with him; a rickshaw boy, "an Indian with skin the color of wood not quite burned to charcoal" whose "name was Charlie also"; and "two boys about sixteen" who invited him to go for a walk "through streets where I would never have been able to go alone in uniform." In his short visit to Ceylon, Charles was able to capture in words its sights, customs, and personalities. He said, "Now that Ceylon is independent there are many less British, but still enough Europeans to keep in existence this sort of separate city and society within the typical Asian turmoil of the rest of the city." He said of the Indian population, "I think they are the most beautiful people I have seen…and I would love to go to India someday, simply because here are people living there full of such grace and good nature."

## 4 July 1954: Durban and Denying Negroes "Status of Human Beings"

Charles described Durban, South Africa, as "quite European in appearance…clean, rather a resort. Afrikaans, a Cajun sort of Dutch, is commonly spoken here, but everyone understands English and it is the written language most commonly seen. Durban is also like Kentucky, however, with its extreme color bar and Sunday blue laws, when all the bars and movie houses are closed up tight as a drum.

"The Dutch farmers look like Pennsylvanians of a hundred years ago must have, stolid and sturdy and religious. The girls are all ruddy and busty, the boys stoutly built and long legged and blond.

"As I imagined, the colored boys on our ship were denied access to any places of business, to restaurants, movie theaters, and the like. They have left the ship only on rare occasions after the first blunt exclusions.

"The South Africans wish they could deny the existence of the 'natives' altogether. Since that is obviously impossible, and since they wish to exploit them in industry, they deny them the status of human beings, pretend they are not there as long as they do not grow too obvious, and hit them if they do…"

Charles said he was pleased by the letter from his cousin Gretel (in response from his and his mother's letters to her): "The tone of this one was not the vague and adolescent tone of the other; she was even a little chastened, I think, full of a more healthy concern with her immediate life and acquaintances."

## 1 August 1954: Final Shipboard Letter; Visiting Rio de Janeiro

In his final letter home from aboard ship, Charles described his visit to Rio de Janeiro, Brazil: "I had a good time there, but three days were quite enough; the buildings are frightening…imposing structures of ferroconcrete, half-empty, some almost erotic, others distorted, in shape. Enjoyed a walk along the beach front; many weird people, intense, mostly unsmiling, the women provocative." He told his parents, "Tuesday (the 3rd) we arrive in Trinidad, our last foreign port, and with any luck I'll be out in two weeks, at most three," and instructed them, "Next time you hear from me will be Norfolk. Don't send any more mail to the ship after receiving this letter."

Charles arrived "home" in Winter Park, Florida, late in August for a brief reunion with Mom and Dad; brother Richard, a sophomore in college; and younger brothers Bill, Jim, and Neil, the "wee boys" who had now become adolescent and preadolescent young men. He was there only a few days before embarking for New York City.

# PART FOUR

# New York City 1954–55

# I

# SEPTEMBER 1954: SETTLING IN NEW YORK, JOB AT BRENTANO'S

In an undated letter from New York City in early September, Charles wrote of his arrival "safe and sound… Got a room at the 23rd St. YMCA—2.50 a day including membership. Subways are 15 cents now. Going up to Columbia today…fees will be payable in advance… I'll let you know just as soon as I can my permanent address." From the YMCA he wrote, "I have a room now—9.50 per week… It is a half block off Riverside Drive on 11th Street… I start job-hunting Monday." Charles made inquiries about study at French language school ("I can take advantage of such a school for free"). He visited his Navy friend Roger Long in the Naval hospital in Philadelphia. Roger was on medical leave with emotional and mental problems.

On September 13, Charles interviewed at Brentano's Bookstore, and on September 15, he began work there—"4th St & 5th Ave., 8:30 to 5 with Friday and Sunday off." Charles was disappointed in Brentano's as a bookstore– "only a poor shade of what it once was… no attempt is made to maintain a stock of out-of-print books of any kind." He enquired at the Gotham Book Mart "up the street" about author Henry Miller—who, he learned, was "still alive at age 60 (in Big Sur, CA, married again)." Charles had obtained copies of some of Miller's books in Orlando, Florida, and was hoping to obtain others in New York.

He hoped to register for classes at Columbia on his day off. He wrote of the number of languages spoken by the Brentano staff and discussed at length the many Puerto Ricans there, calling them "good people—but people without real homes." He said his parents "would not recognize the old avenue, the old neighborhood" (where the Haldeman family lived on Riverside Drive from 1939–41).

By September 24 Charles had registered at Columbia University and been reunited with the Marritt family, who continued to be his gracious host in the city. He had received his first check from Brentano's—"a mere pittance…but I can live on it all right…" Charles wrote of celebrities always coming into Brentano's, including the poet Ogden Nash and the sons of actors Robert Walker and Jennifer Jones, "uncanny images of their father."

In a month Charles had become established in New York City but continued to look into future educational opportunities. He heard from his (Navy) friend at Antioch College who had the same advisor as Charles did—Basil Pillard (who was widely known as a linguist). Charles was also considering returning to Antioch and writing Professor Pillard. He wrote Black Mountain College in North Carolina (a short-lived very progressive school) for information. He lamented that "working 8 or 9 hours a day" left him little time for the language study necessary to study overseas.

Charles assured his mother, "If you are more than nominally concerned about me, relax. If I am to fulfill anything for you or for me or for God, it may take a long time. It may take longer than I live and other people may have to look back for the meaning in it, or the form. But so what. How I go about it concerns how honest I am, how simple, nothing else really."

II

# FRANCES STELOFF AND CENSORSHIP, TEDIUM, HOME NEWS, REUNIONS

In October Charles signed up for a French class at the Ecole Libre ("Free School") "which...is not quite (free)." He went to an exhibition of Henry Miller's watercolors "at invitation of Frances Steloff" (Ms. Steloff, who died in 1989 at age 101, was founder and longtime owner of Gotham Book Mart, which attracted the greatest authors of the twentieth century. She was a strong opponent of censorship).

At the exhibit Charles met Anaïs Nin and Abe Rattner, famed author and painter known for their relationships with Henry Miller. "Both of them were unassuming and I liked them." Charles wrote a long letter home on censorship, especially as it applied to Henry Miller's books, most then banned in the United States. He said Frances Steloff might make a "test case" by openly selling these books. He was considering attending Hans Hofmann's art school but had withdrawn from his course at Columbia as it was "a mess...will get 80% of my money back...a 20% lesson to be learned, I guess." His course at the Free French School was to begin November 1. The remainder of the autumn months fell into a routine, something Charles found hard to abide. He wrote home that he was doing some reading "but don't feel... I'm accomplishing an awful lot" because of his living arrangement and long hours of work. He placed himself on several publishers' lists to receive advance copies of books and asked for a number of books from "home." Letters from home, in which his mother described Haldeman family events, also relieved his tedium.

Frances Haldeman had involved herself (indirectly) in a notorious criminal trial in Winter Park, Florida, providing care for the defendant's eleven-year-old son. She was drawn into this case because Charles's

67

brother Neil, also eleven, was a close friend of this boy. The boy's father was accused of murdering his wife. Charles's comment, "Seems dubious that he shot her," proved correct as the father was acquitted.

A letter from Charles to Mom included his advice for parenting his brother Richard, then a sophomore at Rollins. He suggested ending his brother's dependence on his home and parents. "If he can shift for himself and go to school still—fine… Anything he does is fine—so long as for a change he does it himself. In other words, the same choice I had to make, finally… Whatever is given to someone who takes the giving for granted only perverts the user, I'm afraid."

Richard was not made aware of this letter, nor did his mother follow the advice. He was unaware that he was such a financial burden to his parents, who housed and fed him and provided tuition from Charles Heuss's insurance until he graduated from college in 1957. At the same time, Charles wrote for a copy of a short story Richard had written that was praised by his brother's creative writing professor. In his letters home, Charles also expressed his desire to continue correspondence with his cousin Gretel. Charles's absence from his own family was relieved by visits with the Marritt family, with whom he spent Thanksgiving.

Charles was also being joined in New York by friends from the Navy. He wrote that his artist friend Roger Long "has been dismissed from the hospital in Philadelphia and is in New York for a few days before going to Texas. He is on convalescent leave and he will probably be mailed a medical discharge while he is home." Roger was planning to come to New York following his discharge. Also joining Charles in New York was Navy friend Al McCarthy, who had been studying at Antioch but who left school and remained in New York after Christmas. He and Charles were looking for an apartment, and by the first of the year, they had rented one in Brooklyn, along with a friend, George Smith, who had also dropped out of Antioch.

As Charles had predicted, 1954 had been "a strange year." It began with eight months at sea around the Pacific and closed with four months in New York City.

# III

# ARTISTIC EXPERIENCES, A TRIP HOME,
# VISITING HENRY MILLER

When 1955 began, Charles became impatient to move forward in plans for his education and his life. The only college in America that appealed to him was Black Mountain College in North Carolina (which was to close in 1957). He described the appeal of this college in a letter home: "The only fields for study are the creative ones springing from the so-called 'humanities' subjects: painting, writing, music, language, theater, manual arts of ceramics, pottery, et cetera, and the only degree given is B.A."

Charles was now convinced, however, that his dreams could be fulfilled only in Europe, where he also wished to revisit his German family. He hoped to obtain "employment on a ship crossing to Europe when I go" and to leave in the spring. Before this was to be accomplished, however, Charles was to discover the great artistic and intellectual experiences available to him in New York City.

Charles and Al McCarthy spent New Year's Eve at the home of Oscar Baron, whom Charles met at the Henry Miller Art Showing. Mr. Baron ran the Alicat Bookstore and had received permission from French novelist Louis-Ferdinand Celine to print the author's first novel since World War II. In a letter home, Charles described the controversial life and works of Celine, adding, "yet his writing creatively is powerful & consistent, no matter how pessimistic, and seems to remain so, no matter how little capable he is of so-called 'normal' human relationships." He added, "Anyway—I'm going to do the cover for the chapbook when it's printed— if the translation is completed in the not-too-distant future..."

A few days later Charles attended a cocktail party at the invitation of Frances Steloff of Gotham Book Mart, honoring Harry T. Moore on the publication of his biography of D. H. Lawrence (this biography was later revised and updated in the 1980s). Frances Steloff presented a copy of the biography to Charles, and Harry T. Moore autographed it. Brentano's had purchased an eight-thousand-volume library, and Charles reserved for himself "beautiful editions of John Donne's and William Blake's poems."

Charles's mother sent him an article in *The Nation* by Kay Boyle (the well-known author and political activist blacklisted during the McCarthy era just now coming to an end). Charles had mentioned having met Ms. Boyle at the showing of Henry Miller paintings: "It was in that connection which I was prompted to read her article." Charles wrote his mother of the discussion of the group that night concerning "the position of the artist in American life…and the pressure continually exerted upon him by the average man, who flaunted his 'equality' as though it covered every aspect of his life automatically— simply because he was an American."

During the discussion Charles argued that "freedom for the artist and the intellectual consisted in how much weight and how great importance was attributed to their utterance and their work by the man-in-the-street who cannot claim (as he does here) to have equal knowledge or sensitivity; that the very value of this attitude toward the man of letters and the artist was in its dynamic effect on social life." Kaye Boyle agreed with Charles, "He's right you know. When Monsieur Gide spoke, they all listened, down to the last truck driver." Charles added, "I was very tickled to find that the keynote of her article (in *The Nation*) was the transformation of the contemporary scene into one where 'the voice of the artist, that voice which speaks with such superb authority in France, in England, in Italy, can, if they wish it, become the voice of authority here.'"

At Brentano's a woman doctor to whom Charles gave a copy of Simone de Beauvoir's *The Second Sex* reciprocated by sending Charles "two fine Italian silk cravats" and told him she would also be in Europe this summer. Frances Steloff urged Charles to visit Henry Miller if he went to California. "Maybe I will; she has offered to provide me with credentials."

This whirlwind of activity in January and February also included Charles's personal life. He wrote that the apartment he shared with two friends "seems likely to be only temporary; with three of us in it. It is a little tight; I think we can get something cheaper as well." His friend Al McCarthy was seeking a job; he was financially strapped from his semester at college. Al was getting married in early February to leave only Charles and George Smith in the apartment. Later plans were changed: Charles and George moved, and Al McCarthy and his wife took over the apartment.

The apartment was also shared for a short time by Roger Long, but Charles wrote January 29: "Roger left today—returning to Texas. It was rather foolish of either of us last fall to think he would have been happy here." During this same period Al McCarthy was in Texas to pick up his fiancée, whom he married February 3 in New York. In a letter home written the next day, Charles described Al's wife: "quite attractive, though very young and nervous, red-headed with small eyes—that peculiarly Texas look that almost everyone I know from Texas has." During this same period, the Marritts took Charles to dinner, and Charles described for his family the "nineteen feet (6'3", 6'4", 6'5") of boyfriends" visiting the beautiful Marritt daughters.

As February ended, Charles was able to exult in a letter home: "Good news! My passport arrived today as did also two copies of my birth certificate from Pickens—both in just one week…it means I can get my seaman papers from the Coast Guard this next week and leave promptly after next pay day (I gave notice today) from New York—so I'll see you shortly." In March he was able to leave for a month's visit home with Mom and Dad and his younger brothers. At Easter he met Richard's girlfriend and future wife, Janice.

During this month Charles did travel to California and did meet Henry Miller. Miller wrote in his book, *Big Sur and the Oranges of Hieronymus Bosch*, "My warmest thanks go to Charles Haldeman, who came all the way from Winter Park, Florida, to put Wilhelm Franger's book on Hieronymus Bosch in my hands. May he forgive me for being such a poor host that day." Later Charles was to form a friendship with the author, whom he admired for Miller's unabashed and unbridled expression of his humanity. In his letter to his mother from sea, Charles had said most people were unaware they were alive. Not only was Miller a person "aware he was alive" but he was also one who reveled in life.

# V

## FINAL DAYS IN NEW YORK, TRIP IS ON, MEETING ERIC GUTKIND

Back in New York, Charles indicated he planned to call off the trip to Europe, accept work from Ruth Marritt's sister Alice for the summer, and possibly travel instead to Japan in the fall. His friend Al McCarthy (now married) had written a letter to the Ministry of the Interior in Greece asking about the possibilities of buying property on a Greek island. He received a favorable reply; this was misleading to Charles, who later experienced difficulties in obtaining Greek citizenship (denied) in order to purchase a villa on Crete (this was accomplished through a proxy with later disastrous consequences).

Things had changed four days later when Charles wrote home: "Please disregard what I said in my last letter; I must have been standing on my head. I have bought my ticket; I leave the 29th on the ITALIA to Copenhagen; the ticket cost me $185. The trip takes about eight days, I think." Roger Long was back in town, perhaps to study with Hans Hofmann. He was interested in possibly studying at a Jesuit university in Tokyo Charles had recommended.

Charles and his friends meantime were enjoying the New York City arts scene. The Marritts' daughter Naomi, an aspiring ballerina, had a role in the Metropolitan Opera's presentation of *Othello*. Charles and Roger Long took Janet Collins, chief ballerina for the Metropolitan Opera, out to dinner. Charles later had dinner with the poet Ruth Forbes Sherry, whom he had met in California, and her son, Commander Sherry of the US Navy. On another day he and Roger visited the art class conducted by Roger's teacher, Hans Hofmann.

Of the latter event, Charles wrote home April 24, "That in itself would have made a successful day. But in addition, the same evening Roger, Al, Jennette (Al's wife) and I went to the Gotham Book Mart where Erich Gutkind was speaking to a small group (among which we were included by invitation…from Miss Steloff). The talk was the last of a series of lectures on the Bible and the state of man, much the same theme as The Absolute Collective, the book by Gutkind of which Henry Miller speaks so highly in The Wisdom of the Heart. Dr. Gutkind extended his lecture to include some remarks on Einstein, with whom he had been corresponding at the time of Einstein's sudden death."

Afterward, Dr. Gutkind and his wife engaged Charles in conversation. Charles described them as "exceedingly charming and vibrant, and it was a great privilege and pleasure to talk to them." Dr. Gutkind asked Charles to write him from Europe, and his wife asked him "to say hello to every city in Europe for them." (The Gutkinds had been forced to leave Europe under Hitler. Charles possibly modeled his concentration camp philosopher in *The Sun's Attendant* on Dr. Gutkind.)

This was to be Charles's final letter to his parents from New York City, ending his eight-month sojourn there on a high note. His next letter was to be from sea on the way to Europe.

# PART FIVE

# Germany and Greece 1955

I

# Meeting German Family and Viewing "Monuments to…Stupidity"

Charles spent his last night in New York, April 28, with the Marritts and was shown off the next day by his friends Roger Long and George Smith. He wrote home May 6 on his final day at sea, "We will come to Southhampton, England tomorrow." He described his fellow passengers: "most of the girls on the ship are soldiers' wives going to Germany for the first time, very young most of them." Among his "many acquaintances was a young man from Frankfurt who had been working for his uncle in America and was visiting Germany before returning to the US to enter the Army." Charles said, "He is the most likeable person I have met since I left the Navy."

Ten days later Charles wrote from Trier, Germany, where he was visiting his aunt Erna; her husband, Gustav Feuerstacke; and their teenage children, Gretel and Hans. Erna had formed a close friendship with Charles's mother during Frances's 1935–36 visit to Germany. Gustav, who had been a customs officer before being drafted into the Wehrmacht during World War II, was able to return to this duty following the four-year de-Nazification process necessary to reenter government work. Before moving to Trier, the Feuerstackes lived in Heidelberg, first in Oma Heuss's cramped quarters with Erna's brother Richard Heuss and Richard's wife, Gret, and then in an apartment when Gustav was hired as a custodian in a Heidelberg teacher's college. When Charles arrived in Trier, Gretel (eighteen) was searching for her place in life. Hans, in high school, was an active athlete, participating in track.

Charles had been corresponding with this family, especially Gretel, for several years; and a letter from Gretel to his mother told how delighted she was to meet him. Charles planned later in the summer to take a bicycle trip to visit his uncle Richard Heuss (for whom his brother was named). After a decade of scratching out a living, Uncle Richard, who had also served in the Wehrmacht, was soon to become part of the new West German Army. Charles told his mother of his hope to visit Willi Kuhn (not the politician but probably another friend of his mother's from her 1930s time in Germany).

In Trier, Charles enjoyed swimming in the local public pool. He joined the family in a walk through the ruins of the Roman arena and "up through the hills and the young Riesling vineyards overlooking the city—tranquil and pleasant." Of the ruins, Charles said, "There is something perverse in the preservation of the decayed remnants of the past. There are too many monuments to man's stupidity and cruelty lying all over Europe…one can often not distinguish between the Roman ruins and those of WWII. It would be better if adequate housing for the living were provided for a change. But this is only one of thousands of conflicts between the past and present that tears Europe continually." Charles concluded his first letter from Germany with "But everyone is very friendly and send their love. I'm studying a little German (out of a book) every day."

Charles was enjoying his time with the Feuerstackes. He wrote that he had told Hans that his brother Dick (Richard) was, like Hans, an avid sports fan. Charles enclosed a letter to Richard from Hans, and Richard responded—each writing in the other's language. Charles's letter also included a description of Uncle Gustav: "I rather like Uncle Gustav. I suppose he is a man whose ingrained ideas, or perhaps lack of real ones, are dangerous when multiplied by very many (I guess we have seen how dangerous)—but who individually has a certain kind of cocky, self-possessed charm, in this case emphasized by a rather explosive energy left over from the war.

"Perhaps in him, too, there is a key to a lot of German thinking. I cannot imagine him being as much fanatical about anything as just plain obdurate and set in his thinking—with a quick tendency to categorize and then overlap." With his limited German, Charles was a patient listener to Gustav's monologues, "which are always interesting, whether informationally or revelatory." Charles found Gretel to be "a little bit of a problem, first of all because she is not quite a woman, not still a girl" and "because I think she had speculated much more on me than I ever on her— that is, on what I would be like, how I would accept her, etc." Charles said, "The German is progressing…I'm going through my grammar again, page by page."

Charles's time in Trier gave him time to settle into a routine of daily German study "for the next month or so…whence I shall probably make a bicycle trip with Hans." He had not yet planned his time in Germany: "there is something weighted, penumbrae, about this year for me already." He asked his mother to send peanut butter to surprise Hans, who had learned to like it when introduced to it by Americans in Heidelberg.

Gretel later told Richard how happy her family was with the arrival of that peanut butter: "I remember the peanut butter he gave us, it was something he did as a very nice surprise. I also remember the care package Charlie had sent [earlier after World War II]. We were so surprised, so happy. Another memory: my mother had sewn a summer dress for me, and when Charlie saw it, he asked her if she would make him a shirt of the same material and explained that he wanted the American version (open all the way in front, not like the German one, only half open). She made it for him, and I loved it when we wore the same stuff once in a while."

Charles wrote his American family that he was also using this time to read works of American authors "that I should have read a long time ago and didn't." This led him into a discourse on America and its failure to fulfill its dream: "The American authors I consider really worthwhile— even great—Whitman, Emerson, Mark Twain, Willa Cather, Sherwood Anderson—all write unmistakably about the same America—one that almost but never quite existed except in some particulars. Or as a dream— and not merely what is called 'The American Dream.' They are in love with a spirit that never had a whole body. Yet it is a spirit that does not exist in particulars first. That is—it isn't just an idea. All of them really experienced it, yet they are disappointed lovers—what they found, they couldn't hold onto except by transplanting it into the artificial soil of art… Reading it, I get homesick for this America, that only could exist…"

Charles wrote that he had received two letters from friends in New York. Florenz Baron, wife of Oscar Baron who ran the Alicat Bookshop, sent him Celine's address in Paris, but mentioned disappointingly that her husband would not be publishing the English translation of Celine's book (for which Charles had hoped to do the cover for the chapbook). Mrs. Baron sent Charles addresses of her friends in Rome and Paris who would be glad to meet him. Al McCarthy wrote that Roger Long was also still in New York, working at the New York Public Library.

Charles had written to the man from Frankfurt he met aboard ship about the possibility of making a trip to the Mediterranean with him. The friend accepted Charles's invitation, and on July 25, Charles wrote home of a trip that that was to change his life: "Frankfurt early tomorrow afternoon. Then 3 or 4 days later on our way—will probably stop by a couple of uncles on the way down." Charles felt he had accomplished fluency in German in Trier. He looked forward to "this trip (which will) be different from anything I've done before…"

Charles never possessed an automobile driver's license, but that was not a detriment to his ambition to travel to Greece. He had gained a love of cycling while a paperboy in northern New York and planned to make most of this trip by bicycle. His success in this effort was shown in an August 25 letter home: "We're on our way to Greece, and there's not enough time to begin to see Italy… Next to Naples; it would be nice to catch a boat from there—perhaps work over to Piraeus—otherwise we'll take a train to Brindisi; the stretch between there & Naples is too long & uninteresting to cycle. So far we've made about 1700 or 1800 km.—the last few days from Genoa to Rome were worse than any— uphill and down—and hot… From Athens next letter."

On September 9 Charles wrote from Athens that he had spoken with the Minister of the Interior about his friend Al McCarthy's request to purchase a Greek island. The minister "has an island picked out for Al. We'll go to it when he has time some Sunday. Meantime he's offered to make an itinerary around Greece for me and my friend, complete with letters to the prefects, etc. Too good to be true—but everybody here is like that." Charles also gave a glowing description of Greek food: "nothing I've eaten in the last week was familiar, but everything has been delicious; the Greeks can really cook."

Charles had received a letter of introduction from Henry Miller to George Katsimbalis (the "Colossus of Maroussi" of Miller's book) but had not yet been able to meet him. It was the image of Greece portrayed in Miller's book that had made Charles fall in love with Greece before ever visiting there, and now all his experiences seemed to fulfill that image. He described Italy as "just the opposite. A republic without republicans—dying of dropsy and indigence & dishonesty."

On September 19 Charles wrote from the island of Kos, "two miles" from Turkey: "Tonight we take a boat to Rhodes… This island is…very disappointing after the little island where we spent the last half of last week—Mykonos—called 'the white island'" (This was where Charles was later to live while writing his first novel, *The Sun's Attendant*.) Charles concluded his long beautiful description of Mykonos with "The sea on windy days is the sea of Van Gogh, vitriol blue, white-capped, and the round hulled boats with their exaggerated keels & violent colors are his, too."

Charles's delight in Greece made him discouraged about returning to Germany. Although he planned to be "back in Germany—Munich—about the 9th of October at the latest," hopefully to spend a week with Uncle Hermann, his father's older brother, he did not "plan to remain in Germany more than one other month after I get back." (He was to change his mind about this.) He said he hoped to see "Al's island" by the end of the month—"it lies near Ydra or Hyrdra, not far from the Peloponnese."

Charles wrote that he was now traveling "with another German fellow— from Heidelberg—speaks a little English & the same amount of French. He's a sculptor, studying in Athens—22 years old. We came together from Piraeus."

This new traveling companion, Pieter Sohl, was to become a lifetime close friend, one who helped Charles become established in Heidelberg and study at the university there.

(In 2015, Pieter Sohl spoke of his friendship with Charles at a book fair in Heidelberg, introducing the German translation of *The Sun's Attendant*. By then Pieter Sohl had become a renowned sculptor and was himself subject of a biography. Charles's brother Richard; his wife, Janice; and their daughter Nancy Cochran were able to spend a delightful day with Pieter and his wife, Birgit, in the summer of 2016, two years before Pieter's death.)

In an October 11 letter, Charles described his travels through Greece with Pieter Sohl amid torrential rains and in filthy, leaky boats ("the train costs 3 times as much"). He and Pieter had to get up early in the morning to go by bus, boat, and burros to Athos, where they would gain permission to visit the monasteries. They planned to be in Athos around ten days "if the weather is decent." At Hydra they had encountered a "tropical downpour" that "washed half the mountain into the harbor" and sent "spigots" of water down into their room in an old home. The rain was accompanied by "lightning like instances of daylight over the whole island."

On October 24, Charles wrote, "Yesterday afternoon arrived again in Thessaloniki after a little over a week in Athos... we leave for Athens again today & shortly thereafter for Germany... we had a most interesting time, visited 5 monasteries—met quite a number of rather unusual people, of whom the monks for the most part turned out to be (overtly at least) the least unusual." He described a Greek wedding he attended followed by a celebration in the village tavern where "everybody (or rather all the men— since the women seem to disappear as soon as it gets dark) was drinking and dancing to the music of 4 guitars & two clarinets and a violin—Greek folk music & dances." In another letter Charles related a humorous account of his and Pieter's trying to smuggle a bottle of cognac from Greece.

On October 31, two days before returning to Germany, Charles wrote home: "The experience in Greece has been a rich one—I've seen a lot of places, seen many things, but if & when I finally return, I shall penetrate more into the life than I have been able to do this time." Pieter had helped convince Charles of his need for more education, best obtained in Germany, and Charles stated his intention to return to Germany "after all" and to "make application to enter Heidelberg in April."

Writing from Germany after his return, Charles explained his love of Greeks: "The peace of which Henry Miller speaks is there, & perhaps the people there are the most valuable of all Europeans because they are in no way decadents—they are too poor—they are not feudal, they are in an unconscious (largely) way deeply rooted in the earth— and though they have great faults as a 'people' that are perhaps not to be overcome, that are perhaps great enough to rob them of any 'destiny, ' they are yet lovable, they celebrate life instinctively through the individual."

Charles related the experience he and Pieter had in hitchhiking for 350 km on their way back to Athos. They traveled over Mount Olympus in a wood truck over "a winding, dangerous potted road." The next day they lay "half the day—a beautifully clear and sunny day in Macedonia—in a green field which stretched between the mountains…in full view of Olympus some 15 or 20 km away—a great blunted purple knob of a mountain wrapped in clouds of shifting thickness. We felt greatly at ease somehow, though we weren't about to get a ride for several hours, and we were glad we hadn't gone by ship back to Athens." Pieter had taken a number of photographs of their travels, and Charles suggested that perhaps there was a market for articles he could write to accompany these photos.

Charles had heard good news from his aunt Erna and her family: "Tante Erna & family have been moved, Gustav again in uniform as customs officer on the Luxembourg border; Gretel has a good job with the American Air Force finally. She is happier, earns 5 times as much money as before."

The trip back from Greece was rough, and Charles had to cancel a visit with Uncle Hermann in Munich. He wrote in November 1955, "back in Germany—in Heidelberg—I didn't stay in Munich. Pieter was sick the whole way from Greece on the train, rain and snow in Yugoslavia, only Austria and the Alps yet beautiful; it was foggy and damp in Munich. When we got there it was almost 8 in the evening & we decided to come on to Heidelberg."

Charles made a quick trip to Frankfurt and Trier to pick up his clothes and papers and hurried to Heidelberg to attempt to register (late) for the fall semester. He hoped to receive an exemption from the requirement that American students have two years of study before matriculating. If not, he might still be able to attend classes as a *gasthoerer* (guest auditor) and receive GI Bill benefits. He looked forward to study at Heidelberg, though he still had reservations about staying in Germany. He wrote home, "I think I'll like Heidelberg, although I can in no way revise what I have said already about Germany: the life lacks an interior, the young people here are beaten and all the energy goes out the window or else into the same stereotyped channels as in America."

Later he wrote from Heidelberg, "Germany is like I knew it would be—cultural concerns wrapped up in overcoats. The river dripping frangible and mercurial through its slices, easing like a grey python round the bends. The beautiful fall is over, and now everything is the same color. But it fits the people: when they don't have little things like coal and potted plants to worry about—they aren't happy. God help me if I can't get back to Greece next summer."

## II
# BECOMING NONMATRICULATED STUDENT;
# KINDNESS OF SOHL FAMILY

On November 21 Charles reported good news to his family; he had been accepted as a *gasthoerer*. Though "nonmatriculated," he was "able to collect full GI Bill... I'm taking mainly philosophy—a couple of literature courses...and my hours are fine—nothing before 10 AM—and every Saturday & Sunday free." He praised the Sohl family for helping him settle in Heidelberg: "Have an overcoat too, courtesy of the Sohls, who have literally broken their backs being nice to me. I have a sort of room, too, but must look for something better—because this one is cold. (You can use the Sohls' address...until I am really established)."

In a later letter, Charles described Pieter Sohl and the Sohl family, which he compared to his own. "My friend Pieter Sohl...is going through very much the same business as I did in 1950, wanting to be at home and yet knowing the time was very shortly coming when I should have to go away once and for all, and not be a member of a family any real sense any more. It is making a great many problems for his mother, as it did for you... The thing is complicated because the type of family from which he comes is so very unusual, especially for Germany, also five children, three younger sisters and a brother, and all very much of a family not in the German patriarchal sense, but like a little liberal democracy.

"He loves it and so nobody is saying to him in the slightest 'You must go away.' He simply knows it is time, if he is to be a sculptor he has to get beyond the child-exercises; he has talent and sensitivity, but in the end he just isn't quite ready to measure up to himself...right now his father is perhaps too patient, and his mother fights with herself because she finds it difficult to be patient enough."

83

Charles continued to hear from his friend Al McCarthy in America, whose wife was now pregnant. Al expressed concern about Roger Long who still "doesn't know what to do with himself" though he could be "the greatest painter in America. He suffers from aloneness." Charles himself was "in a fog… I shall go crazy, or else suddenly without a word to anyone pack up & head back to Greece." He had a new address (in Ziegelhausen "permanent?") and "started moving today."

Later his mother wrote him criticizing his continued concern and preoccupation with Roger Long and his "running away" and holding his "individuality aloof." (It is unfortunate we do not have Frances Haldeman's letter to Charles.) Charles replied that rather than holding his individuality aloof, "I have done something almost diametrically opposed: I have been stewing it all over the place. Now the learning I must do in the next few years is to concentrate it… I have known, I have felt for a long time, that my 'critical' intelligence is not an analytical intelligence…I must generate and not electrocute. This running away business is like a short circuit…but give me time, I will come through."

In a December letter, Charles expressed his impatience to begin to "generate." He described his "brainstorm," to write a screenplay from D. H. Lawrence's *The Man Who Died,* to be filmed in Greece with the cooperation of persons he met there. "I should be able to make the necessary contacts to produce the thing, poets, scriptwriters, photographers, whatnot. Frances Steloff of the Gotham Book Mart in New York would assist me I'm sure in laying my scenario in the hands of Lawrence's widow in New Mexico for permission to produce a film from the book. Ah, maybe it's all a pipe dream, but I won't know until I've tried." (Charles later wrote numerous screen plays; sadly, none were produced.)

Charles rented a typewriter and asked his mother to sell his typewriter in America to help pay for a large shipment of books he was requesting to be shipped—seventeen volumes, largely philosophy, psychology, poetry, and biography. He also asked for three Henry Miller books, "if you can get them in." In another letter Charles showed that preparation for his writing career included the storing of personal as well as reading experiences. He described his landlady in Ziegelhausen: "the widow of the cousin of (the anthropologist) Leo Frobenius…an aristocratic woman in rather reduced circumstances, living largely in the past... Her husband was killed in the first world war and her son in the second. Her grandson she raised herself after he war; he is now sixteen and in Munich with an uncle. Her son, whose pictures she showed me, was a poet, thirty when he was killed, and evidently of some promise. All I know is that he had a beautiful face... expressive and sensitive and strong, and I shared her sadness a little."

At the university, Charles found German students harder to understand: "strange and over serious and isolated, the boys much worse than the girls. I suppose it can't be helped, but it makes things more irritating than they should be. Thank God there are some nice French students here and that I have a few friends like Pieter Sohl... otherwise there would be no one to who I would even so much as open my mouth. There wouldn't be any point to it."

By December Charles had received his resident's permit and was awaiting his GI bill compensation for his studies at Heidelberg University. He wrote home December 28: "Already a week of vacation...Had a pleasant enough Christmas, dinner with the Sohls, dinner and a little Christmas eve party with the family I live with. Got a box of cookies from Uncle Willy and family. Tomorrow I go to Ettlingen to spend New Year's with Uncle Richard and his wife, Gret." Willy (actually 'Willi') and Richard Heuss were younger brothers of Charles's father; Gret (Margarete) was Uncle Richard's wife. (Decades later Tante Gret; her son, Joerg, a young boy in 1955; and Joerg's family were gracious hosts to Charles's brother Richard and his wife, Janice, on three trips to Germany.) While settled in Heidelberg, Charles was already looking forward to returning to Greece, although the GI Bill wouldn't transfer his credits there. He wrote, "By the time summer comes, I should have enough money to go back to Greece for a couple of months before returning in November for the fall semester."

Thus ended 1955 for Charles Haldeman—a year beginning in New York City, continuing in Germany with reconciliation with German relatives he had met briefly as a young child, finding its high point with a trip to Greece and a friendship formed with Pieter Sohl, and closing with his enrollment at Heidelberg University as a nonmatriculating student who felt like an outsider. Despite his feelings of low accomplishment, Charles had made personal, literary, and artistic contacts in New York, in California with Henry Miller, and in

Greece and Germany that were to enrich his life and enable his career as a writer. His language study and voluminous reading had prepared him to study at a great university. His attitude toward life and study in Heidelberg were to improve greatly when classes resumed in January 1956.

# PART SIX

# Heidelberg University 1956–57

# "Everything Is Going Well" with Heidelberg Study

When classes began again at Heidelberg University, Charles wrote home January 13, 1956, that "everything is going well—finally." His books had arrived, and his GI Bill payment for Heidelberg had been approved. He had secured a "decent, cheap room" in Heidelberg, one of the most expensive cities in Germany, and was overcoming "the last vestiges of difficulty with the (German) language." He wrote, "I am enjoying most of my classes very much, working until 3 or 4 every morning." He put his Navy service to use to earn an occasional free meal by peeling potatoes in the student café. He was taking lessons in Greek from a Greek student at the university and hoped to "hitch hike back down this summer to Greece for the vacation, and practice what I've learned."

In a January 18 letter, Charles told his mother of his frustration in finding enough time to write: "Right now my hours are too irregular and I have too much reading to do, to work writing in." Still he was working on a screenplay, possibly based on the D. H. Lawrence book, and planning to write short essays on Greece and work on some short stories. His study of Greek was progressing, though he realized how difficult learning that language would be. Charles passed on some studying advice to his brother Billy (Willard Haldeman Jr.) who was to take an examination to enter Kings Point Merchant Marine Academy. Billy passed the exam and later graduated from Kings Point. Charles exhibited his descriptive ability again in telling his family of the young German man with whom he might rent a room. The man lost a leg at the end of the war while still a teenager. He was an aspiring painter who had returned from an aborted trip to Africa as companion to a middle-aged American couple from Louisiana.

At the end of January, Charles wrote that his first GI Bill check had arrived and that in February he might move to the city with the German man he mentioned in the last letter ("about 26 years old, he lost a leg in the bombing at the end of the war"). Instead of spring vacation in Sweden, Charles was considering "April in Paris" with a French girlfriend. (She, Caroline Aubrey, was to figure in his and his family's lives for years to come.) Charles had found a new, easier-to-study Greek language text. He wanted to "stop reacting to this winter in the way that I have," describing its icy cold in ten colorful negative adjectives and an obscene analogy (this from a person who spent six years in northern New York State, which has probably the worst winters in the United States!).

Charles moved into Heidelberg—"no more midnight trips to Ziegelhausen"—despite "10 below zero, a little snow—lots of ice." He had been to the dentist, replacing "amalgam fillings of the last 18 years." "I shudder to think of what it's going to cost me, but it's not so expensive here as in America." He received a letter from his American friends Al McCarthy, whose wife was expecting a baby, and Anne Marritt, "a good sophisticated, intelligent girl." All the Marritt children had turned out well.

Charles had applied for a translating job in Stuttgart. In late February he wrote, "I heard from the firm in Stuttgart; I have a free hand, can work as much as I like and demand the fee that I want…in the next month or two I can pay for all the gold that's going into my mouth." Charles also praised his new apartment—"warmer and centrally located…between two of us it costs no more than the other one with me alone in it." He enjoyed swimming in the city pool. The weather, both in Heidelberg and throughout Europe and the Mediterranean, remained in deep freeze.

Charles lived next door to the Amerika Haus where he was able to read current American newspapers and magazines. He read William Bradford Huie's story in Look magazine about the murder of Emmett Till in Mississippi and criticized Huie's cold reportage of this event and also in Huie's previous book, *The Execution of Private Slovik*. He said Huie's dispassionate writing "never transcends the research. I have the continual impression that he is telling nothing but lies with every documented fact that he writes." In one of his notebooks, Charles wrote his own account of this event, attempting to add meat to the bones of Huie's account.

When his brother Richard, who had worked two summers on daily newspapers, wrote him defending the objectivity of journalists, Charles replied, "That which is called 'factual' occurs only in a context from which the reporter cannot, dare not, stand off, without having made a lie of what has reported. Every crime is a crime of the general conscience, in which we participate by our objectivity." In this, like the previous, letter Charles went on for several paragraphs criticizing Huie.

# Spring in Greece and Paris; Fully Matriculated Student

In early March, Charles began his spring vacation, giving him time to begin his translation job from Stuttgart. He reported that he had "earned $35 in 3 days—in the next two weeks I shall be doing translations to the tune of about $110. An unexpected windfall with no visible end." Spring was on its way: the snow was melting, the wind was warming, and there was an occasional rain. Charles's future also began to come into view. He wrote that he hoped to be "instated as a fully matriculated student for the fall—in the case that I am, I will remain in Germany one year more." That ambition was to be realized.

At midmonth Charles planned "to escape Heidelberg for a month, perhaps not to France but to Greece." Three weeks later, it was from Greece that he wrote, "It was the best possible idea to come…spring in the air; the air is so dry and clear that it carries the sea in it in little pockets—vigorous—the sea always there in it to smell." By completing three translations in six days and being paid $100, Charles was able to pay for his trip to Greece. He looked forward to the opportunity to witness the burial ceremony of the Archbishop of the Greek Orthodox Church—"a once in lifetime occasion. He will be carried through the city, sitting, fully clothed in his robes of state in the Archbishop's throne, to his grave—a morbid grandiose spectacle— unlike any other in the world."

Later Charles wrote that the archbishop's funeral did come off with the expected pomp and ceremony, viewed by "3/4 of the population of Athens." He added, however, that the government had forbidden "the body's being carried upright after the old tradition." Charles's sharing of Greek prejudices and verbal involvement in Greek politics, that were later to cause him problems, were also expressed in this letter. He discussed the critical situation in Cyprus, where he doubted "there's a single Greek who doesn't want Enosis (union) with Cyprus." He criticized the British and American "noncommittal" position and said "the life or death of NATO" could depend upon resolving this issue and added that British attitudes "are either direct expressions of bad faith in Greece or a pretending that Greece simply doesn't exist."

Charles had made a new friend in Greece, Christos; and together they planned a trip to the islands or to Olympia. Stating that he viewed Greece as an artist, not a tourist, he described the Acropolis under "a perfect blue sky—the marble comes alive—like live rock though, not live something else." He said those viewing the Acropolis by moonlight have "invented sensations to fill the space… God created marble in broad daylight and tourists by the light of the moon." His artistic muse aroused, Charles asked his mother to send him all his poems she could find. Refreshed by the trip to Greece, he also looked forward to returning to Heidelberg on April 24. He told his mother, "Greece has…put some distance between me and this last winter… Heidelberg won't be half so bad in summer, I suspect."

Even while in Greece, Charles continued to write of personal matters. He wrote to Erskine College—which he attended and where third cousin, Dr. Mauldin Lesesne, was president—and to Rollins College, where his brother Richard was a junior, asking about possibility of Caroline Aubrey attending as an exchange student. "It will be fine if something comes of it." Caroline had contacted both schools. She was accepted by Rollins, which she attended in 1956–57, spending much time with the Haldeman family, where Frances Haldeman treated her like the daughter she never had.

Charles's study at the university for the summer term was interrupted in May by the Pfingsten (Pentecost) holiday. He was enjoying the swimming pool—"the weather is magnificent"—and had a new room in "the old house that Pieter Sohl has rented…cheap too." His girlfriend, Caroline, was visiting; she had heard both from the president of Rollins College and the visiting French teacher there who would be in Paris in June to interview her. He was completing his dental work, "very extensive, inexpensive by American standards, and permanent."

Charles told of visiting the family Vogel, friends of his grandmother Heuss. He wrote his mother, "Frau Vogel asks to be remembered to you— asked about 'Dicky' [his brother Richard, a baby when Frances, Charles and Richard visited in 1935–36]. Her son is married now— her daughter-in-law there with two small children—a friendly, very German young woman." Charles closed his letter with a description of postwar Germany: "Time is fractured for the Germans, the war & its end still seem like an immediate yesterday—whereas when they speak of the 'Hitler Time,' they could as well be speaking of a historical period at least as remote as that of Frederick the Great. The cleavage of conscience is complete and the two phases of Late Germany are written in two different books that are never laid side by side on the same shelf." Perhaps that explained the strangeness of the German students with whom he was studying at Heidelberg, later known as "war children—the forgotten generation," torn between these "two phases" of German history.

Charles utilized his vacation to fix up his new room and complete his Stuttgart translating job. He wrote, "Things are going much easier in the university this time," and he was making an application to be taken on as a regular student in the next semester. Charles received his income tax refund in time to finish paying for dental work, which had rid him "of the remnants of the work of about 15 childhood dentists." The news from Cyprus continued to concern him: "The English couldn't be making a bigger mess of it—possibly. The Americans are coming in for a lot of criticism they don't really deserve." Charles said Americans are unable to comprehend or understand "how unpopular we have gradually made ourselves in the world." (The end of colonization and deepening of the Cold War—the Suez crisis was still ahead—made 1956 a year of conflict, and one in which America's postwar popularity was quickly fading.)

As the holiday ended, Charles visited his girlfriend, Caroline, and experienced Paris in springtime "with less than $10." He wrote, "It was a wonderful week. Hitchhiked there & back." Coming home he and his German friend on the trip were luckily picked up by an American soldier who was able to arrange for them to sleep on the base "then send us farther on with a school bus the next morning—it was damned nice of him." He sent home a photo of Caroline and one of Roman, the German student with whom he had hitchhiked to France—"the most pleasant Heidelberger I've met."

Caroline Aubrey later visited Charles in Heidelberg for ten days, and Charles wrote, "She will definitely be coming to Rollins sometime in September." He assured his mother, however, "I'll let you know when I am 'serious' about a girl. As far as concerns Caroline, I like her very much— perhaps more than any other girl I have met in Heidelberg— but that is as far as it goes, and I am entertaining no intentions about the future."

Charles's translating work for Stuttgart paid his rent, made a payment on his dental bill, and paid the first installment of his university bill that semester—enough "to last me until the first GI Bill check comes the end of the month." He was planning to host brother Richard's girlfriend (future wife), Janice Hamilton, later in the summer; and he asked that she be forwarded instructions of how to find his apartment. He sent news of the young German whom he met on the ship to Europe and with whom he later took the bicycle trip to Greece. The man was now settling in America, and he asked his parents to be his host if he ever came to Florida. Charles sent congratulations to brother Billy (Willard Jr.) on his acceptance to Kings Point Merchant Marine Academy.

In late June Charles sent a four-page handwritten letter home complaining of late GI Bill payments, the government's treatment of veterans studying overseas, US foreign policy toward Greece, America's treatment of African Americans, the refusal of a passport to playwright Arthur Miller, and the general failure of America to honor its ideals. He criticized the low GI Bill coverage of veterans studying abroad, the delivery of checks months late—"I have been living on 45 cents a day for 3 weeks now"—and the Veterans Administration administrator in Europe who resented Americans studying there. Nevertheless, he was determined to continue his studies at Heidelberg: "I am afraid if I interrupt now I shall never start again." He said his education in Europe "is worth so much more to me than any kind of security or 'future' that America could possibly offer me... If I had to come back for long I would die, in my soul."

Charles continued his discourse with a discussion of Greek-American foreign relations. He said that every Greek has "the ideal of America," which was suffering from American foreign policy toward Cyprus, NATO, and England; the civil rights struggle in America (the

Montgomery bus strike); and the refusal of a passport to playwright Arthur Miller. Charles concluded, "The Greeks are the one people in the world today who will forgive us our money, our brashness, our youth, our pushiness; but they are the last people in the world who will allow themselves to be bought and sold or used politically."

In late July, Charles wrote with good news: "I have been accepted as a regular student in the next semester, on the strength of my 3 semesters in the States and 2 semesters as guest-hearer here." In that same letter Charles made his first reference to Renate Gerhardt, to whom he was later to dedicate *The Sun's Attendant:* "In September a German woman here and I will make an adaptation for German TV of a story by Herman Melville, which we expect to be able to sell for $400-$500. Here's hoping."

Widow of the poet Rainer Gerhardt, Renate was to be the model for a major character in *The Sun's Attendant.* In a July 11, 1960, letter to Charles, Renate described their relationship during that 1956 summer and fall: "I remembered the days in my tight, rain-cold quarters during that summer which was as rainy as the present one…the night during which we, four or five lying on the floor, followed Eisenhower's election; our parties in the living room; all of these became present again, strangely transformed and all at once in a somehow meaningful relation."

In the summer of 1956 Charles also awaited a visit from Richard's girlfriend, Janice Hamilton (Jan), revisiting Germany for the first time since she lived there from 1946–49 as the daughter of an US Army occupation officer. Charles wrote, "Heard from Jan out of Austria. She'll be coming about the sixth of Aug." (Janice was traveling with her Austrian friend Edith Partik, who later married Alois Mock, the future foreign minister of Austria. Edith had been an exchange student at Janice's high school in New Rochelle, New York.) Before their arrival, Charles planned a short visit with Gret and Richard, his aunt and uncle, in Ettlingen. He reported wonderful news from the university: "Through one of the professors here I have received a summer stipendium of 250 Marks (60 dollars) which was a sudden pleasant surprise."

On August 7, Charles wrote, "Jan and her friend Edith Partik are here, came are here, came day before yesterday—busy making visits and seeing things. They are staying here in the house—Pieter (Sohl) and his wife are in Spain." Charles entertained Janice and Edith and other friends for supper and a late evening. He had received a letter from Al McCarthy with photos of Al's baby daughter "who doesn't have red hair, like his wife—he's a bit disappointed." Charles's mother had written about the movie *The Strange One,* being filmed at Rollins only a block from the Haldeman home in Winter Park. Charles described for her the novel and play *End as a Man,* on which the film was based.

After his visitors departed, Charles was able to leave on a long planned trip to Holland. He had purchased a Youth Hostel card and told his family the itinerary of his three-week trip—"Otterloo, Amsterdam, Rotterdam, probably Brussels, visit Caroline's family shortly in Lille and come back over Paris."

# III

# TRIP TO HOLLAND, FINAL DAYS IN GERMANY

Charles wrote on August 23 that he was enjoying his visit to Amsterdam. He was staying at the home of Johan Somervil, with whom he had worked with at Brentano's. Johan was now foreign representative for a publisher and distributor for paperbound books in Holland. Charles said, "He has treated me so royally while I've been here that I'm practically at a loss for words of gratitude." He praised Amsterdam as "a very beautiful city with its old buildings and canals, both of which are lighted at night... Most of my time has been spent walking and in museums—also in reading. The museums here are absolutely fantastic, so many van Goghs...and the Rijksmuseum is full of Dutch masters and Spanish... The Dutch are for the most part quite reserved but very friendly. They still distrust and dislike the Germans more than any other people than (except) the Danes."

After sending his parents a long list of books, food, and clothing to send him, Charles apologized in a September 10 letter: "It dismays me to see what I've asked you to send here; just send basically what you can and I'll be satisfied with that." He wrote that his girlfriend, Caroline, would arrive in Winter Park, Florida, to attend Rollins College on "the 25th or so." Caroline Aubrey had asked Charles to thank his mother for writing Caroline's mother to reassure her about Caroline's upcoming trip to America.

He and Renate Gerhardt planned to take their TV script to Stuttgart "and we'll know after the visit pretty certainly what our chances are to sell it... I'm pretty hopeful about it, because it is really good." A week later he wrote that the project "progresses well, even hearteningly—considering neither of us has ever done anything exactly of the sort before." He and Renate were going to the International Book Fair in

Frankfurt, and Charles's friend Johan from Amsterdam would represent his company there.

Unfortunately, there are no remaining letters home from Charles during October and November, so the fate of his and Renate's script is unknown. That his mother wrote of her concern about his dearth of letters during this time is indicated in his letter to her December 13. He reassured her of his well-being, stating that he was not "suffering or in any way intrinsically unhappy…or that anything I may be doing is incommensurate with my capabilities or my sensitivity—or that there is anything you could be doing more than you are."

Charles also addressed her continued concern that he had absented himself from America and remained determined to make his life in Greece. He wrote, "Getting to Greece is for me no 'escape from the boredom of Germany'—but a reality I love far more than I shall ever be able to love that America which exists as vision & possibility but not in the flesh." He said he had "genuine affection" for the friends he had made in Europe but that "whatever nostalgia I've had for my childhood" has been "smelted for a long time, until it has become an enduring and valid part of my adulthood."

Although he had not been home for Christmas for seven years, Charles wrote, "As long as it's no longer possible to come home & then to come right back—I don't even think about it." He turned down a Christmas invitation from Caroline Aubrey's parents (he could not afford the trip) and asked if he might visit instead at the end of the semester. (Interestingly, Caroline spent that Christmas with the Haldeman family in Winter Park, where Frances Haldeman had become like a second mother to her. Except for Charles, all the Haldeman sons were home that Christmas—including young Bill, a freshman at Kings Point, along with their cousin Carolyn Cantrell, a college junior later to become a high school French teacher. Diabetes was to take her life ten years later.)

Charles's decision to remain in Heidelberg for Christmas proved a good one. He wrote January 7 that he had "got more done in the last two weeks than in months before—mostly reading, or catching up on correspondence…a very satisfying & restful holiday on the whole." He added, "Heidelberg is at its best, such as it is, when it is not so 'international.'" He described many students as "fish out of water when they get away from their native lands; they display only their cruder sides in any milieu than their own… I think young people have a very strong & unavoidable reliance upon a strong indigenous culture pattern, & very few are certain enough or open enough to be able to live in an amalgamated environment such as this."

Charles enjoyed his visit with a German archaeologist friend who cooked "healthy food—baked beans—instead of the pork and potatoes diet most Germans eat." Charles said this was "understandable for the first 7 years after the war" but "no longer excusable." Charles's plans for the immediate future now seemed settled: he was to leave for Greece in March (after visiting Caroline's parents and his uncle Hermann and family in Munich) and then "conceivably…go on to Vienna for a week and visit Eddie (a friend of Jan's from Rollins) and Jan's friend Edith." He had decided against a job offer from his friend in Holland as "I am so confident that, given two years in Greece, I can realize so many things both intellectually and spiritually."

In a January 21 letter, Charles expressed thanks to his mother for helping to make these future plans possible. He wrote, "I'm somewhat at a loss to say anything about what your last letter meant to me. What you're making possible for me carries advantages with not only for the next year, but also for some years to come." He said he was "heartened…even liberated" by her "sacrifice." "Thank you from the bottom of my heart, both for the freedom and the responsibility." (What his mother was promising was probably funds from his father Charles Heuss's insurance and possibly additional funds to become established in Greece.)

A week later, he expressed his love for his mother even more fully. He thanked her for sending the books he had requested ("I know it's a hell of a nuisance digging the books out…if anything at all justifies the trouble…it's the genuine pleasure and feeling of contact I have when I get them"). Then referring to the family problems that had caused her to carry "the world on your shoulders for too long," he wrote,

> As for me, please don't ever think I've been anything but aware and thankful for the kind of woman and mother you are, even at these moments when my awakening grasp of myself, or a sudden intense need to feel isolated and independent have seemed to remove me from you, or to estrange us in some

way. You are always in my heart very close to me, and it is this essential closeness, this bond of understanding, that allows each of us to lead radically separate lives without ever losing touch where it is most important.

For Frances Heuss Haldeman, whose widowhood had left her with the care of Charles as a child in the Depression-ridden and war-looming world of the 1930s, these letters from her twenty-five-year-old son must have been precious possessions.

On February 21, 1957, Charles wrote his final letter home from Heidelberg: "Either Tuesday or Wednesday I'll be leaving Heidelberg … traveling quite light for having been almost two years in Europe… just the two suitcases and the footlocker holding about everything I own in the world. I'm full of happiness and anticipation…this jump is going to have great meaning for me. I'm sure of it." He had introduced his landlady to pecans (sent from America). She said he'd been lucky to have the room "because it looks out over the river on one side and on the other onto the old bridge and its tower, on the university side."

He concluded, "A few people that I still have to visit, and then the ties with Heidelberg will be pretty much broken off." Charles's life adventure was just beginning. His next letter, dated March 6, 1957, was from Greece, where he would spend the remaining twenty-six years of his life, a life that would end just six months after that of the mother to whom he was so close. His life in Greece was to begin with fulfillment of his literary promise and to close in tragedy.

# PART SEVEN

# Settling in Greece, Success as Author 1957–74

## I
# ATHENS, 1957–60: TEACHER, MATHEMATICIAN, ARTIST, LYRICIST

On March 3, 1957, Charles arrived in Greece, "bag and baggage." There, despite the lack of academic credentials, he so impressed the staff of the Anglo-American School that he was hired as a teacher of biology and algebra. His colleague there and lifelong friend, mathematics teacher Jim Yeros, remembered in a letter to Charles's brother Richard, "He came to Greece from Germany riding a bicycle." The two young teachers became, in Charles's words to Jim, "foxhole buddies," spending "many hours investigating prime numbers," following Charles's "obsession with finding the prime number pattern." Later Jim Yeros married and had two sons and provided Charles with a surrogate family. Charles also began a close friendship at the Anglo-American School with Byzantine scholar and linguist Harry Hionides. When Harry, later a professor at Athens University, became a husband and father, Charles also became close to his family.

This need for family contrasted with Charles's determination to express his individuality and to connect with the Greek and international literary community. It kept him grounded during the next two years while, as he later expressed in an "Outline of Life in Greece," he "seriously studied Greek, began outlining his first book" and "made a broad variety of acquaintances and lasting friends, among them Nikos Gatsos and Odysseas Elytis the poets, Mano Hadjidakis and Mikis Theodorakis the composers, Nana Mouskouri the singer, Yannis Tsarouchis and Nikos Hadzikyriakou-Chika the painters, as well as old 'foreign hands' Phillip Sherrard, Edmund Keeley, Kevin Andrews, Mark Ogilvie-Grant—to name only a few." He described this as "an exciting time to be in Athens, and I was extraordinarily fortunate to land there when I did." During this period he used his artistic training to record Athens street life with a group of pen-and-ink drawings still in existence. His friend, artist-sculptor Pieter Sohl, praised the attention to detail in his drawings: "No one could draw hands like Charles."

In 1959 Charles left his teaching position to prepare himself for a writing career. In his "Outline of Life in Greece," written in 1982 during the final year of his life, Charles described the 1959 and 1960 years: "I traveled three times to Crete—a new experience altogether—and revisited Mount Athos, spent two months in Turkey, mostly in Ankara, not long before the fall of Menderes, met Lawrence Durrell at the Gypsy Festival in Stes.-Maries de la Mer, and went on to spend a week with him and Henry Miller in Nimes… got to know, in large part through Nikos Gatsos: Peter Levi, Gregory Corso, Allen Ginsberg, Elia Kazan and a great many other well-known people who were either already connected with Greece in some way, or whose lives brought them there during this remarkable period. I would mention none of them, either, if each had not in some way left his imprint on my life, whether in passing or in durable friendship, and had not contributed something to my perception of how Greece affects greatly disparate sensibilities, while remaining virtually impervious to their attempts to offset it."

During this period Charles was also devoting himself to writing. In a July 11, 1960, letter, Renate Gerhardt told him, "You have just completed a great piece of work and I send you my very special admiration for it." She was obviously referring to a film script as she said she planned to submit it to "the head of our theatre-section…who manages the film and broadcasting rights for our House [the publishing house for which she worked]." She continued, "In any case, for heaven's sake, do not give your script to anybody! Not until it is protected!… Would the subject matter be suited to a book edition? We are always after good things." The title and fate of this script is unknown; and it was, unfortunately, never filmed.

Charles was, however, experiencing success at that time in another writing field. Academy Award–winning composer Manos Hadjidakis chose him to write the lyrics—both in English and German—for the title song for the Twentieth Century Fox movie *It Happened in Athens*. During production of the film in Athens during the fall of

1960, Charles met both the star, Jayne Mansfield, and cast member Bob Matthias, American Decathlon Olympic champion. In addition Charles portrayed a member of the American 1896 Olympic team in the movie, with one spoken line! Unfortunately, the film was a critical and financial failure although the title song, with Charles's lyrics, has been recorded several times since by leading female vocalists. (Charles later exhibited his ability as a lyricist and playwright when he wrote the book and lyrics for the musical play *The Golden Wings*. With music by Vassilia Dimitriou, the play was performed throughout the 1973 summer season at the Ancient Theater of Piraeus.)

Though he was still an "unpublished" author as the 1960s began, Charles Haldeman had made a large group of friends and connections, both in Greece and among the international literary community, that were to serve him well as a writer. In a stroke of fortune, largely engineered by his mother, his stepfather, Bill Haldeman, was assigned by the US Air Force Base Exchange to Bitburg, Germany, in 1961. This also made it possible for his mother, Frances, to return to Germany and reunite with the German in-laws she had befriended in 1936. His parents' finances were now stable, and they were able to provide him financial assistance, a second "home" in Germany, and time and privacy to write. He found this time and privacy on Mykonos, where, in early 1962, he settled down to write.

II

# WRITING AND PUBLISHING THE SUN'S ATTENDANT, 1962–63

As raw material for his novel, Charles brought to Mykonos memories of people and experiences from his South Carolina childhood and adolescence and his university years in Germany. Brief as those German years were, they provided Charles the opportunity to meet many members of Germany's wartime generation and its "forgotten generation," children who grew up during the war. Among them were his close friends Renate Gerhardt, editor and translator and widow of the poet Rainer Maria Gerhardt, and artist Pieter Sohl, who grew up in the midst of the World War II firebombing of Germany. He had also heard wartime experiences of four German uncles who served in the Wehrmacht, established a keen interest in the European Gypsy communities, and been intrigued by the German Jewish philosopher Eric Gutkind, whom he met during his months in New York City. How could these disparate experiences be brought together in a book of fiction?

To do so, Charles chose as protagonist for his novel the German gypsy Stefan Bruckmann, whose mixed identity, age, rootlessness, and vagabond life mirrored his own. The time of the novel, the midtwentieth century, was contemporary to Charles's life, though the novel's setting was principally Germany–Weimar, Nazi, and postwar—rather than America. The lives of the author and his protagonist do come together in the South Carolina and Heidelberg episodes of the novel. The novel is described as a "diptych" (a writing tablet with two hinged leaves), which provides a means for Stefan to bind together the parts of his history just as the novel provides means for Charles to do the same. The concentration camp sections feature a philosopher, possibly modeled on Eric Gutkind, and the Heidelberg section includes experiences

105

of the widow of a German poet, based on but not entirely true to those of Renate Gerhardt. Stefan's experiences in South Carolina are based on—sometimes closely and sometimes distantly— Charles's experiences and college life there. The South Carolina soldier who adopts Stefan—Moon—shares some characteristics and experiences of Charles's beloved Uncle Waddy McFall, though many character traits and all tragic events regarding this character are fictional. The American student at Heidelberg University, John Kallergis, mirrors Charles himself and his views of World War II and its aftermath. In *The Sun's Attendant,* he has Kallergis express these views:

> No, I don't know what it's like, and as I'm always being told, I was too young at the time to remember the last one. After all, I was only ten when it began and fifteen when it was over with. Besides, being an American, I am automatically excluded by nationality from any discussion about what it was really like… But I'll tell you something: I do have something to say about the war, or I will. It has to do with conscience…It is people like me, brought up the way that I was and in the place I was, people for whom the war was very far away and yet unimaginably close, sentimentally, affectively close, ubiquitous. It prodded us continually, as a condition, inescapable, whispering to us in as million ways about its existence out there, as an It…we felt the coloring of it in everything around us, more intensely every day as we grew—and now it is people like me who are its only accumulative children, the only people, or almost the only ones now, who are still concerned with that big It, who have to be, who still have the war unresolved inside them, and know it has to be resolved if we are to go on to anything at all.

Charles was near completion of writing this novel when Jonathan Cape publisher Tom Maschler visited Mykonos in 1962. At Jonathan Cape, Maschler was responsible for purchasing Joseph Heller's Catch-22 and for publishing such authors as Gabriel Garcia Marquez, Ian McEwan, and Bruce Chatwin. He was captivated by Charles's novel, to be titled *The Sun's Attendant;* and in October 1962, Jonathan Cape accepted it for publication. In February 1963 Charles wrote his parents in Bitburg: "The American contracts have been signed and are on their way back to New York… I've finished my blurb and my autobiographical data, sent the photographs and my reactions to the first set of editorial queries, and that wraps up everything." In his "Outline of Life in Greece," Charles recalled the novel's "acceptance by Cape during the Cuban Missile Crisis." Ironically, it was shortly more than a year later, in November 1963, that *The Sun's Attendant* was published. Like the missile crisis, this coincided with another world-altering event, the assassination of US President John F. Kennedy. Charles dated the autographed copy of the book he mailed to his brother Richard "22/11/63."

Charles had earlier mailed a copy of the manuscript to Renate Gerhardt, to whom the book was dedicated, for possible German publication. Renate wrote him October 4, 1963, "The manuscript of *The Sun's Attendant* fell upon my head like a millstone. A dedication with which I am be presented as a surprise, a plot which tries to incorporate important parts of my private life, an author with whom I am joined in good and cloudless friendship, a style which demands of the reader the same effort that exacts of himself, and a respectable volume of a manuscript…this book has simply blocked me for the moment, has smitten one with dumbness, and that I am perplexed at your propagating it as…the dead and, therefore, defenseless Rainer's biography, which after all it is not."

Renate wrote again December 4, 1963, after seeing Charles at the Frankfurt Fair, where she told him, "I was immensely thankful for the understanding which you displayed." She explained further her difficulties in dealing with the book: "I hope to God that you have understood the quite unliterary reasons for which I cannot produce the book myself. I could no longer take pleasure in life if the negotiations with my mother-in-law regarding Rainer's texts, which until now have good prospects, would fall because of a matter like this. After all, it has taken me ten years to reflect on the organizational misfortune of my losing the authority over the estate" [the estate of poet Rainer Marie Gerhardt, who had committed suicide in 1954].

Although the book was also published by Simon and Schuster in New York and in twelve other countries, it was not to be published in Germany for more than fifty years. Renate Gerhardt's reluctance to publish the book probably had less to do with its nonpublication than the German "economic miracle" of the 1960s. With West Germany's economy and infrastructure rebuilt and with its becoming an integral part of NATO, German publishers probably saw little audience in Germany for a novel reliving the Hitler years, concentration camps, and the hard times during and immediately following World War II. The Simon and Schuster dust jacket summation of the book—"Mr. Haldeman has given us…a fascinating portrait of Western society at the middle of this century"—spoke of a period many Germans wished to forget.

Excerpts from the novel appeared in periodicals preceding its publication in Europe and America. *The Paris Review* published a chapter, "Man is a Wonderful, Woundable Animal," in its Summer-Fall 1963 issue; and *Harper's Bazaar* included a section of the book, "The Story of Mushkar," in its March 1964 edition.

In nations where *The Sun's Attendant* was published, it received lavish praise from many reviewers. Charles's friend, author Lawrence Durrell with whom he shared a similar personal history, called it "a moving and evocative book." The most glowing review was from *The Times Literary Supplement* in London: " To finish a new novel by an unknown author with a sense of complete satisfaction is rare. To come across one that compels instant second and even third readings is far rarer. *The Sun's Attendant* suggests itself as something more than a fresh and accomplished work of fiction. It arouses the kind of puzzled excitement that can sometimes mark the entrance of an outstanding writer. At the very least, Mr. Haldeman has a most original mind and a set of unusual gifts." In concluding his review for the *Saturday Review,* William Gibson pointed to the important role of the concentration camp holy man in the novel, asking, "How many novelists of this century have reminded men that they may be holy men?"

At the end of 1963, with proceeds from the book and assistance from Tom Maschler, Charles bought a bomb-ruined Venetian home, Angel One, near the harbor in Hania, then the capital of Crete (Charles always spelled the city *Hania*, rather than its more traditional spelling *Chania*). Due to Greek law, this purchase was possible only through a Greek proxy, Nikos Stavroulakis, an artist and his former colleague at the Anglo-American School. Stavroulakis was an American, born in Wisconsin and educated at Notre Dame and the University of

Michigan, whose Greek parents gave him citizenship in Greece and who claimed Jewish heritage that enabled him to live and work in Israel during the 1960s and early 1970s. This proxy purchase was to sow the seeds of tragedy for Charles, but in 1964, Angel One became his home for a decade, during which he established himself as a citizen of Hania and enjoyed his most productive decade as a writer.

III

# A Creative Decade, 1964–74: Author, Film Writer, Magazine Editor

During the spring and summer of 1964, with advance money for his novel and contributions from Maschler and Stravroulakis, Charles began restoration of Angel One. The film *Zorba the Greek* was being filmed in the harbor at Hania, and Charles was alternately supervising workers, writing his second novel, and enjoying conversations each night with filmmakers, actors, local dignitaries, and expatriate artists at the Kavouria Taverna. At the end of the year, however, Charles encountered the first of many difficulties that were to plague him for the remainder of his time in Greece. With no reason given, he was asked to leave Greece.

Charles had this order rescinded after presenting his case for three months in Athens. Five more such orders were made over the next decade before he succeeded in receiving clearance from the Greek National Security Agency once and for all. It was not until 1980 that Charles felt he had discovered who was behind this defamation. Not only did the Ministry of the Prime Minister clear him the first time in 1964 but it also sent him on a fact-finding trip to Western Thrace and Cyprus to investigate Greek relations with the Turkish minorities in those places.

During this trip Charles was able to repudiate charges of mistreatment of these minorities and to share a private conversation with Archbishop Makarios, "who among other off-the-record revelations concerning the Queen Mother of Greece, John Foster and Allen Dulles, and John F. Kennedy, accurately predicted the downfall of George Papandreou almost five months in advance" (Charles Haldeman: "Outline of Life in Greece"). Upon return, Charles attempted to sell editors Tom Maschler and Bob Gottlieb on book dealing with Greek-Turkish relations, a subject they thought lacked an international audience.

Charles did not shy from expressing political opinions. He was always on the side of Greece in international disputes, though Greece's unstable government made it difficult to take stands on internal affairs. His outspokenness was to raise suspicion and help create later problems with his attempts to gain Greek citizenship.

Despite all these diversions, Charles was able to complete his second novel, *The Snowman,* for publication in 1965. Based on Charles's childhood and teenage years in Sackets Harbor, New York, the book had as its protagonist a Greek-American boy, John Kalergis, who had first been introduced to readers as a student at Heidelberg University in *The Sun's Attendant.* It painted a vivid picture of prewar and wartime life in a small Army town with a utopian former communist, his deaf-mute daughter, a war-wounded poet, and a Jewish doctor intruding upon the conventional life of longtime residents.

*The Snowman* was much more autobiographical than Charles's first novel, and the town's Jewish doctor was largely modeled on Dr. Sammy Marritt, wartime physician in Sackets Harbor. Dr. Marritt and his family remained close friends with the Haldemans even after moving to New York City. The Marritts opened their home to Charles each time he resided in or visited the city.

*The Snowman* also garnered fine reviews. Robert Nye wrote in *The Guardian,* "Haldeman has followed up his exciting first novel, *The Sun's Attendant,* with a work equally original and decidedly more profound. Here, maybe, is a major talent in the making; no American novelist since Faulkner strikes me as having a finer awareness of the possibilities of language as an index to the complications of human behavior; which is to say that Haldeman is worth reading for his sentences as well as for what the sentences add up to."

Charles's publisher Tom Maschler praised it as "a beautiful book… every bit as good (as *The Sun's Attendant*)—possibly better." He wrote Charles in November of 1965, "Books like yours bear children in other minds and will I know in mine, for we are all of one mind if we but realized it and occasionally make this visible. If you end with a voice fallen from the heights…I have it as a sign that the sacrifice was performed and that it will bear…its own fruits in those of others. A blessing on your spirit Charles as upon mine where, in the synagogue of the poet, we all absolve each other." (These words of personal and literary admiration contrasted with Maschler's later rejection of Charles's final novel and his view that his literary work had indeed "fallen from the heights" due to distractions of Charles's life in Greece.)

In the 1960s, however, more success seemed on the horizon for Charles. In the summer of 1966, he was host to film director Christopher Miles and collaborated with him on a film scenario entitled *Nicholas*, to be filmed in Crete. Twentieth Century Fox offered $2,000,000 up front for the screenplay. Unfortunately, Fox withdrew the offer in April 1967 following the colonels' military coup that caused it to cancel all filming in Greece. The film was never produced. Charles collaborated in the summer of 1967 with American composer Francis J. Brown, then living in Greece, on a musical play set in Hania. Charles took this play to New York during his 1967–68 visit to America. (Though he was unable to find a producer there, the play was later performed in Greece with music by a Greek musician in 1973.)

During his trip to America in 1967–68 Charles was reunited with his entire family for Christmas in Myrtle Beach, South Carolina, where the Base Exchange had transferred Bill Haldeman after his six years in Germany. While in America, Charles watched President Lyndon Johnson announce on television he would not run for reelection in 1968 and personally witnessed Martin Luther King's funeral in Atlanta. His written account of the latter experience has been lost.

Charles returned to Crete in 1968 with great expectations for both his creative and personal life. In late December, he wrote to his parents, "Christopher Miles' parents came to Hania for Christmas and I really laid a feast on: from shrimp & crabmeat cocktail through to home-made fruit cake, with easily the best turkey & stuffing I've ever prepared. Mark Nichols (you remember: the bearded publicity director from 'Zorba') also showed up unexpectedly; and Dorothy Andrews was there, with the widow of Herbert Sokow, the ex-editor of Fortune; and Henry Miller's old friend Betty Ryan (the first line of The Colossus of Maroussi: 'If it hadn't been for a girl named Betty Ryan, I might never have gone to Greece'). I am now a citizen of Hania, and if things continue on their present good route I should have dual American-Greek citizenship by spring. All my friends here have been most enthusiastic in their support, and I feel tremendously heartened by it. For one thing (to mention only one) the house will at last be secure."

Charles had embarked on his third novel, *Teagarden's Gang*. A scathing satire of twentieth-century American life, this was a radical departure from his earlier books. The protagonist, Jake Teagarden, was a Prohibition-era gangster with a formula for quickly producing alcohol; and the novel spanned the twentieth century years between the wars, taking the reader to dark places in American politics and entertainment and satirizing utopianism and hypocrisy in high places. The novel was published in 1971 by Jonathan Cape but turned down by Simon and Schuster. Possibly this was due to the criticism of the FBI and inclusion of a principal character too closely resembling J. Edgar Hoover, who was still alive and heading the agency.

In an October 1971 letter to his parents, Charles provided an almost two-page résumé of the theme of the novel, reading in part, "my entire purpose is to render the present day reader conscious of the deeper 'global' roots of present day 'American' concerns, almost every one of which had its first flowering in the years between the two great wars... Hollywood is dead, but films are not; prohibition is gone, but prohibitions are not; rotgut has given way to bad trips on LSD and progressive addiction; Al Catrazzo [the mobster boss in the novel] has been devoured by the Mafia;...and the murderous dream of Utopia is as near as the next Manson commune." (The Manson murders had occurred two years before.)

In the same letter Charles praised Mario Puzo's recently published *The Godfather*, stating, "Seldom has a book swept me along as it did" but adding "But I do not accept its romantic apology for its ultimate hero." He added that Puzo's earlier novels, *The Dark Arena* and *The Fortunate Pilgrim*, "are *infinitely* superior to *The Godfather* in every human, moral, and literary respect" despite the fact that "they flopped where *The Godfather* succeeded." Charles said he would never write "just to satisfy a publisher's idea of what the poor public wants or needs—or to have a commercial hit."

Sadly, *Teagarden's Gang* was to be Charles's final published novel and a commercial failure, though some critics appreciated its satire and humor. Robert Nye of *The Times* praised it as "a competent and entertaining piece of work." Julian Symons of the *Sunday Times* called it "maniacally zestful…unmistakably talented rhetorical writing." Few readers or reviewers, however, captured the depth of meaning Charles intended for the novel.

Beneath the satire and "extraordinary adventures" of "clowns, anarchists, spiritualists, bootleggers, and film stars" that are described in its dust jacket, *Teagarden's Gang* questioned a "peaceless world" in which nations "justify war as a school for life." A central character, Ethel Thurston, a poet's widow and head of the Thurston Society, might well have described the twenty-first-century world when she asked, "If in a peaceless age all is actually war in one form or another, why attribute more significance to one mode of conflict than to another? Of course, there are those who feel that the show of heroism and self-sacrifice and the speed-up of scientific research are sufficient grounds for preferring the open conflagration to internal combustion. I don't agree: Why should the environment of the abominable be a prerequisite for a more frequent manifestation of admirable human qualities?" She later describes the people and nations of the world as "conflicting architects able to build isolated units of marvelous beauty and power, but unable to achieve an overall harmony of design."

In addition to publication of *Teagarden's Gang*, the year 1971 brought news of Charles Haldeman's success in yet another field, writing for documentaries. His and filmmaker Basil Maros's film *The World of Icons* had just captured first prize in the documentary field at the Salonika Film Festival, and they had signed contracts with BBC and Bavarian TV to do a documentary on the history of the Greek stringed instrument the bouzouki.

Maros brought Charles news of their documentary's success at Charles's fortieth birthday party on September 27, 1971, attended by "all my old friends." Also helping to make this event a high point of Charles's life were his expectations that he would write lyrics for all the songs on an LP being prepared by a major Greek composer and that publisher Tom Maschler would advance him $1,500 for a "Greek novel" he was beginning to write. Whether the LP was made is unknown; the novel was later turned down for publication. But as Charles reached that landmark birthday, he could look back on eight years in which he had published three novels, completed a screenplay and musical play, and written the script for an award-winning documentary—all while restoring a bombed-out villa in Hania.

During these years he had proved himself a valuable citizen of Hania. He donated his novels and a rare series of German periodicals to the Hania Public Library, supported the order making the old port an archeological domain, helped to arrange purchases of Cretan handicrafts by the Smithsonian Institution and Hallmark Foundation, assisted in rescuing a prominent citizen from drowning, worked with producer Basil Maros in filming ceremonies commemorating the thirtieth anniversary of the Battle of Crete, and negotiated the transfer of the entire library of Basil Papadakis (diplomat) to the Hania Public Library.

Charles opened Angel One up to leading literary figures from throughout the world who were visiting Greece. He formed friendships with English authors Peter Levi and Lawrence Durrell and American author Henry Miller. He was an admirer and close friend of George Psychoundakis, author of *The Cretan Runner,* a memoir of his years as a Greek resistance fighter working with the British during World War II. In 1972 Charles applied successfully as a private individual to the Ford Foundation for a grant to enable Psychoundakis to continue with his translation of Homer's Odyssey into Cretan dialect.

Despite his contributions to this community, Charles was called in five times during his years in Hania to explain to authorities why he should not be deported. He was asked why he was in Greece and why he wrote in English rather than Greek. Because his writing income came from foreign sources, he was accused of removing money from the country. Charles answered that he loved Greece and the Greek people and found this was the place his creative talents could thrive. He wrote in English because he could best express himself in his native tongue. His writing income was actually bringing money into Greece. No, he was not a CIA agent (many Americans in Greece were). In fact, Charles was becoming "Greek," speaking and corresponding in the language to Greeks. He had even applied for Greek citizenship, but somehow these papers never reached the proper authorities. (Charles's incomplete final novel, *The Arkadhi Alphabet,* describes these events.)

Charles maintained good relationships with others in the expatriate population in Hania, many of whom became friends with his parents on their visits there. These included an Irish couple, the Hogans; a photographer, Carol Martin; and two aspiring writers. One of these was Carol's partner Ted, an ex-CIA agent who later worked for New York City Mayor John Lindsay. Ted (Edward Whittemore) was later to publish five novels, including four that gained some critical acclaim, as *The Jerusalem Quartet.* The other writer was a former US foreign service officer, Allan, an unhappy homosexual dissatisfied with his life and unsuccessful in his writing. Nikos Stavroulakis, in a letter to Charles's brother, Neil, described Allan as "quite ugly, short, wealthy, an aspiring poet." Although Allan was shunned by much of the expatriate population, Charles, and later Charles's mother, showed him kindness. (This was definitely the impression gained from Allan by Charles's brother, Richard, who went with his mother to meet Allan while visiting Hania in 1972. Stavroulakis, however, remembered Allan as once receiving "really vile verbal abuse" from Charles. Allan, sick drunk at the time of this incident, might have been receiving a "fatherly" scolding from Charles, a reprimand out of concern rather than anger.)

Two other persons had close but unusual relationships with Charles. He extended friendship and a job in his home to a troubled Greek youth, Costas. He provided lodging in Angel One for Lee Rediadis, a brilliant, many-times–married editor, for her help in editing and in managing the house. Alexandra Fiada, with whom he later edited *International History Magazine,* described Ms. Rediadis in a letter to Charles's brothers Richard and Neil:

> Lee was intelligent and charming, interesting (had led a very adventurous life…having fought in the International Brigade in Spain in 1936), entertaining, knew all the right people, a good talker on almost anything, and an excellent listener. Since her divorce from her fourth husband she was taking in lodgers. What would have been more desirable for Charles but to stay at her house whenever he was in Athens?

Charles reciprocated by allowing her to stay at Angel One when she was in Hania. He began a strange, close, but nonphysical relationship with Lee that was to last the remainder of his life.

Lee's letter to Charles's mother, Frances, in 1966 gives a glimpse into this relationship and problems Charles encountered as a landlord.

Writing to "Dear Fran," she describes her role in evicting a problem tenant:

> You may not be sorry to hear that I have been instrumental in producing a final break in the…situation. She seemed to me to taking over Charles's house—he being too kind hearted… to protest… She's moving out on Monday and I'll then be moving back in… Charles is starting on a new book and doing some fine writing. You'll be pleased to hear that he is very well, aggressive and impossible and charming as ever. I do so enjoy being with him.

The letter also tells something of the financial arrangement Charles had for restoring the house: "Matters re the construction of the house also are going ahead with the help of new funds from Maschler, who will not be here until August this year which gives Charles extra time to get the place ready." Apparently Charles's coinvestors in Angel One, Tom Maschler and Nikos Stavroulakis, kept rooms in the house as part of the agreement, though Stavroulakis was absent from Greece for most of the 1960s.

The success Charles encountered from 1963–71 continued for three years afterward, despite problems caused to artists by the colonels' government from 1967 to '74. Charles and Basil Manos produced another documentary, *New Roads,* released in 1972, and the documentary film *Bouzouki,* finally released in 1974 after being held up by the colonels' government. Both documentaries were filmed partially in Hania. Charles's musical play *The Golden Wings,* originally written in 1967, was performed in 1973 at the Ancient Theater of Piraeus.

The military coup, which prevented Charles's film play of *Nicholas* being produced by Twentieth Century Fox in 1967, created problems for Charles from both extremes of the political spectrum. The coup delayed some of his projects but created the opportunity for the *New Roads* documentary, which seemed to identify Charles as a supporter of the regime. To his brothers Richard and Neil, Charles's political ideas were difficult to comprehend. Though always drawn to liberal principles, he refused to consider the colonels' regime as worse in its treatment of human rights than previous governments and tended to regard all Greek governments as impediments to the freedom of thought that had drawn him to Greece. Years later, in his "Outline of Life in Greece," Charles reassessed his view of the coup:

> I let my political conscience dowse in its immediate surroundings. Just as almost everyone else in Greece was, I was jolted by the rape of the Polytechnic and the harshness of the new coup that followed. A very painful process of reassessment began for me, and it is still not over.

Frances and Bill Haldeman came to Hania in 1972 to help Charles with restoration, and that summer they were joined by Charles's brother and sister-in-law, Richard and Janice Haldeman. David Holden, chief foreign correspondent for *The Sunday Times* of London, had just left Angel One; and Charles's family was fortunate to receive copies of his new book, *Greece Without Columns*. During two weeks that summer, Charles took the family on a tour of Crete, highlighted by viewing Minoan ruins and by visits with George Psychoundakis (*The Cretan Runner*) and George Kitsambalis (*the Colossus of Marossi*). Family members met Charles's friends, Greek and expatriate, and enjoyed delicious meals, often cooked especially for them. A letter to her mother from Janice Haldeman described Angel One as it was during her and Richard's stay there in 1972:

> Charlie's house is essentially an apartment house consisting of three apartments in 4 floors. We are in the third floor—but the apartment has two levels—that is—there is a bedroom upstairs (which we use) and the downstairs has a large kitchen, terrace, bathroom & bedroom. Mom and Dad (Frances and Bill Haldeman) use the bedroom and Charlie sleeps on the terrace. The two downstairs apartments (1st and 2nd floors) are occupied this summer by a blind man and his 4 daughters… they cook and keep house for their father… In October a new tenant will occupy the lower apartment and Charlie will move into the middle one.

Janice explained, "There are three apartments, one which Charlie has planned for his own use (2nd floor) and two others to rent. They all open onto outside steps and have balconies.

"The loveliest spot here is the view at night from the terrace. The lights around the harbor shine in the water in all colors of the rainbow—all of the taverns are open and people sit outside at the tables which are brought out and the back in each day."

While restoring Angel One and enjoying life in Hania, Charles was busy preparing to enter yet another literary field. Alexandra Fiada, a young Greek editor, was hired by a publisher to serve as executive editor of a proposed "international history magazine." In 1969, she hired Charles to prepare a dummy copy of the proposed magazine. By 1972, after she had turned down several editors proposed by the publisher, "whose English, though their mother tongue, was worse than mine," she convinced the publisher to ask Charles to edit the new periodical. He accepted, and in 1972, Charles and Alexandra began a professional collaboration that was to grow into a personal and romantic relationship lasting the remainder of Charles's life.

Compiled and edited in Greece and published in Switzerland, *International History Magazine* was a monthly magazine containing more than ten articles and features each issue in its usually more than one hundred pages. Color and black-and-white illustrations accompanied stories. Charles and Alexandra not only edited but also often wrote articles for the magazine, which covered a wide scope of world events and people throughout human history. Though it lasted fewer than three years, the thirty-four issues of the magazine made significant contributions to the field of history.

After seeing his family off in the summer of 1972, Charles moved to Athens to prepare the first issue of *International History Magazine* for January 1973. He was there with Alexandra in December 1972 when he received terrible news of a killing in Hania. The former American foreign service officer, Allan, whom Charles had attempted to help, had apparently tried to seduce Costas, the youth Charles had befriended. In the confrontation that followed, Allan may have died of a heart attack, though Costas implicated himself in a "murder" by slitting the throat of a possibly dead man.

Alexandra later described the effect on Charles of this terrible event: "Charles had a terrible feeling of guilt (which never quite left him) because he believed that were he there the murder wouldn't have taken place. He was probably right." Unfortunately, the killing was later misrepresented as occurring in Angel One and being performed by an axe, neither being true.

This tragic event was to be the precursor of troubles ahead for Charles Haldeman. In 1974 Nikos Stavroulakis returned to Greece from Israel and laid claim to Angel One, beginning litigation over the house to last the remainder of Charles's life. *International History Magazine* was experiencing difficulties that were to cause cessation of publication in late 1975. A decade of literary achievement was closing for Charles, and years of wandering and frustration were about to begin. These began at the close of 1974 when Charles began his most extended trip to America in almost a decade.

# PART EIGHT

# Homeless Wanderer, Death in Athens 1975–83

I

# THE LOSS OF ANGEL ONE, AN AMERICAN SOJOURN, MORE LOSSES

In 1974, after years in Israel, Nikos Stavroulakis returned to Greece. According to the accounts he gave in correspondence with Charles's brother Neil, he found Angel One occupied by undesirable tenants, had difficulty in securing his rooms for friends, found the restoration work to be poor, and was insulted by Lee Rediadis, who told him, "This is Charlie's house." He said he asked for but failed to receive return of his original $9,000 for the "initial work on repairs" and said the house was a "write-off as far I was concerned."

He told Neil Haldeman of the problems he had encountered as (proxy) owner of the house following the murder of Allan by Costas, who "had been living in the house and had even been arrested in it by the police."

In 1975 Stavroulakis secured an "expulsion order" for Charles to leave Greece within forty-eight hours. Although Charles was successful in having this order recalled, Stavroulakis occupied the house while he was in Athens, beginning litigation over ownership that was to continue for more than seven years. (Charles was to die January 19, 1983, less than a week before the January 25 "final" hearing on Angel One was scheduled.)

Stavroulakis omitted and distorted many facts and events in the history of Angel One according to the account of this history Neil Haldeman received from Alexandra. Basing her letter on information on Stavroulakis being compiled for court proceedings, Alexandra wrote:

> He (Charles) bought the house in 1963, paying roughly $1,700, by signing precontract agreements in his name. Crete being frontier territory, no foreigner is allowed to own property there unless he gets special permission, or he gets a Greek

straw-man to sign the formal contract; the Greek in his turn has also to sign another contract stating that the property in fact belongs to the foreigner.

After noting that Stavroulakis volunteered to be "the straw man," Alexandra's letter continued: "In the summer of 1964 the secretary to the then Prime Minister…called him (Charles) in Chania (Hania) and told him that the permission had been signed that very day and would shortly arrive at the Prefecture there. However, Charlie never got the permission, and therefore Stavroulakis went down to Chania and signed the final contract, which made him legal owner of the house. He did not sign, though, the second contract, and during the next ten years he kept promising that he would and that Charlie had nothing to fear from him."

Alexandra pointed out that although "Charles tried in vain to trace the whereabouts of that permit," he was unable to give it full attention "because he was engrossed in writing his next two novels and in restoring the house." He put all the money he had earned "plus hours and hours of hard work" into this restoration. During this time he also applied for Greek citizenship "seven or eight times…which would enable him to get the house in his name without any more ado and despite the contract signed by Stavroulakis. The answer was an expulsion order."

Alexandra explained that "a few years after the purchase of the house," Charles was told the reason the second contract had never arrived. He "learned from one of the functionaries at the Prefecture that the permit had arrived but people from the Greek C.I.A. removed it… We pieced the details together after 1975. Stavroulakis, at the time the house was purchased, had first of all a very good and very crooked lawyer (and)…a friend in the military (who during the junta became head of the Greek C.I.A.)… The lawyer on the one hand advised him not to be a fool and sign the second contract, because after the statute of limitations would be over, he would become *de facto* owner of the house; and the man from the Greek C.I.A. took care that a) the permit was removed there and then (in 1964) without trace, and b) that Charles was expelled from Greece at (almost) regular intervals… They drummed up so many accusations, which they put in his file during the junta (according to a good friend of ours who is in the

Greek F.B.I., Charlie's file is the largest after those of the leaders of the Greek Communist Party!)

"Then, in 1975 (when the statute of limitations was over) Stavroulakis… launched an all-out attack. First, he sent Charles, through his lawyer…a letter saying 'Pack up your things and leave my house.' Second, a formal expulsion order was issued, and Charlie was told to leave Greece within 48 hours." Alexandra and other friends intervened for Charles with the general who was head of the National Security Agency, and "the order was recalled and in the future Charlie would not have any trouble in obtaining residence permits."

In the meantime, however, Stavroulakis had gone to Hania, occupied Angel One, and declared ownership. The case deciding ownership of the house went from court to court until (and just after, Charles's death) Stavroulakis was declared owner. Establishing a Jewish museum in Hania, he became a leading figure in Crete, especially among visiting tourists.

On Nikos Stavroulakis's death in 2017, he received a glowing obituary in the *New York Times* and was cited in many obituaries as a "Renaissance man." If Alexandra Fiada's account of his obtaining ownership of Angel One is correct, he was also a Renaissance man in the Machiavellian sense. He gained ownership of Angel One—a valuable piece of property by 1975—with minimal initial payment for repairs and little or no contribution to its further restoration. He ignored financial interest in the house by not only Charles but also by Tom Maschler. The one thing left to Stavroulakis's protection in the home, Charles's collection of books, was later found strewn along a highway in Crete.

Alexandra Fiada questioned the claims by Stavroulakis to be Jewish and to have descended from a Hania family. These claims, accepted by Greek authorities, gained him privileges both in Greece and Israel, where he even assumed an Israeli name. Alexandra said Stavroulakis had told Charles years before, when they were both teaching at the Anglo-American School in Athens, that to be Jewish "would be to his advantage in his life." Alexandra stated, "I do have, among Charles's papers, the birth certificate of Stavroulakis. He was born of Christian Orthodox parents, originating from Mani in the Peloponnese, and had no connection whatsoever with Crete… His father's SECOND wife was Jewish…he concocted a whole saga, maintaining that his father was from Hania."

It was through these claims and his proxy ownership of Angel One that Nikos Stavroulakis was able to occupy the house, declare himself a descendant of the Cretan Jewish population displaced by World War II, and establish a Jewish museum in Hania. Though the latter accomplishment was a worthy one, Stavroulakis's new identity, celebrity, and home in Hania were gained at the expense of Charles Haldeman.

As litigation began over the house in late 1974, Charles traveled to America, where he spent several weeks with his parents and brothers in America attempting to refocus his life in case he was forced to leave Greece. He also hoped to secure help in his legal case and backing for his writing projects.

Bill and Frances Haldeman were retired in Waveland, Mississippi, in a home that young Bill Haldeman, a Merchant Marine engineer, had helped them purchase. Young Bill was sailing out of New Orleans but living with his wife and baby daughter in Northern California. Richard, his wife Janice, and their three children lived in Due West, South Carolina, where he was on the staff and she on the faculty at Erskine College. Jim was a Coast Guard officer working in Washington, DC, and living with his wife in Virginia. Neil, the youngest brother, lived with his wife and stepdaughter in Ann Arbor, Michigan, where he worked in information technology at the University of Michigan.

Charles took an extended trip throughout America with his parents, first spending several weeks with his brother Bill Jr. and his wife in Marin County, California. He used this time to visit friends in California, including Henry Miller, and to attempt to find a market for two film scripts, a documentary on Nikos Katzantzakis and a film on *The Odyssey.*

Charles next spent a couple of weeks in Ann Arbor, Michigan, with his youngest brother, Neil, and his wife. Surprisingly, Charles found in Neil the most kindred spirit among his brothers and formed a relationship that was to be renewed in correspondence and later visits to Ann Arbor in 1975 and the 1979–81 years. In an unpublished memoir, *The Difficulty of Dying in Greece,* Neil wrote of being reunited with his oldest brother in 1967, the first time he had seen him since he was "eleven years old, except in occasional photographs." He was staying with his brother Bill in Baltimore when Charles arrived there to be driven to Myrtle Beach for Christmas the following day. On seeing Charles for the first time in years, Neil remembered:

> I was thrilled. By this time Charlie's first two novels had been published. He was a hero to me, and just a year prior to this he had written to our mother, "I loved Neil's letter & hope he writes me directly soon; the strange (or not so strange) thing is that he manifests the most direct maturity of all: What he has been through (a disastrous teenage love affair, what you have helped him though) has given him the courage of his emotions rather than the mere courage of his convictions...remember that final scene in the film about the Sullivan brothers, who all went down on the same ship in WWII, where the youngest one goes running across the clouds after the others, shouting, 'Hey, wait for me!' Well, Neil doesn't have to shout that any more; he is at least in stride and maybe possessed of just a little more unspent strength."

In addition to his visits to Ann Arbor, Charles maintained a regular correspondence with Neil the remainder of his life. It was Neil that Lee Rediadis telephoned when Charles died, and it was he and his brother Richard who traveled to Athens following Charles's death. After Charles visited Neil in 1975, he joined his parents for a visit to his aunt Vesta and brother Richard in South Carolina. Grossly overestimating Richard's journalistic connections and influences, they asked him to write newspapers to consider hiring Charles as a foreign correspondent, someone few newspapers now employed. (Frances had already written the *Times-Picayune* in New Orleans, and Richard wrote one letter to a retired foreign correspondent with whom he had an indirect connection. Neither letter received a reply.)

Before returning home, Charles visited his brother Jim in Virginia. There is little record of that visit except that it was during Jim's failing marriage and his wife disliked Charles and his cooking (Charles prided himself as a chef!). Charles would have been able to travel to Washington, DC, during this time; but there is no record of this.

In the summer of 1975, Charles returned to Greece. While he was working in Athens, Stavroulakis moved into and claimed Angel One, an event described by Alexandra Fiada in a letter to Neil Haldeman: "When Charlie returned from the States…barely a month passed before he was rendered homeless and in danger of expulsion from Greece. From then on started the merry-go-round of hearings and trials, of rounding up witnesses and friends, etc. Charlie had no 'home,' nowhere to really settle and write as much as he wished to, very little money (and sometimes none at all) and a great load of worries and frustration."

In early 1977 Charles looked forward to a break from his work and writing. His parents were to visit him, and afterward, he was to accompany them on a trip to Wales, where Frances hoped to learn about her and Charles's family ancestors. Charles's fortunes seemed to be on the upswing in 1977. Little did he anticipate that would instead become one of the darkest years of his life.

The visit to Wales had to be cut short when Bill Haldeman, who had enjoyed robust health into his late sixties, suffered a serious illness, later diagnosed as throat cancer. This cut short the trip, causing Bill and Frances to return to America for surgery that cost Bill his voice box. Then, upon his return to Greece, Charles learned that his friend from Anglo-American School days, the Byzantine scholar Harry Hionides, was going to New Orleans for cancer surgery. Hionides died there September 24, 1977. Finally in December 1977, Charles was informed that another close friend, *London Times* correspondent David Holden, had been murdered in Egypt while covering the Middle East peace talks.

# Years of Personal and Artistic Frustration and a Canadian Film Project

For the next year Charles was able to remain in Hania, moving from one cheap residence to another, often exchanging work for his lodging. His Irish poet friend Séamas Carraher remembers first meeting him in 1978 in a "café on a harbor front in Hania." He told of this experience in a letter to Richard: "Charles was living in a rented apt. above an 'upmarket' taverna across from his favorite restaurant in Hania, Ta Kavouria, whose owner was a great friend of his… I was living on the beach nearby before the rain came, looking for work as a laborer, and had just sold a warm jacket to buy wine and bread for myself and Josef, a Swiss-German boy who was also homeless at the time."

Charles came over to their table and introduced himself, putting them at ease when they learned he was a local resident and writer. Learning that Séamas was a poet, Charles invited him and his companion upstairs to continue their conversation in his apartment. "At that time I carried a book by Henry Miller as my constant companion," Séamas recalled, and after he learned that Charles knew Miller, their conversation continued "through that first night, talking of what I can't remember but probably about writers, poets, Henry Miller, and the oppressive state of life that it is the role of writers to point out can be changed ('the world to come' described by the concentration camp rabbi in *The Sun's Attendant* often comes to my mind when I think of many of our conversations)." The next morning Charles gave Séamas an advance on his proposed work. For several days following Charles visited his table and enquired about his welfare, "without," Séamas pointed out, "any criticism nor mentioning that I had even been paid in advance."

That began a deep social and intellectual friendship that was to last the remainder of Charles's life. Séamas described Charles to his brother Richard as "a loyal friend and passionate writer, who understood that the part of literature and 'art' that has the greatest integrity is the life lived with integrity and commitment that is the basis for it." The young poet seeking to discover and express himself as a writer must have reminded Charles of himself two decades before as he left America for Germany and then Greece. In letters he wrote to Séamas in 1979, he urged the young man to get his drinking problem under control, assuring him, "You are an exceptional person, no matter how much of a muck the world is in—and you cannot, must not, drown in the surrounding slime…Get that teaching certificate, get anything you can that puts solid ground under your feet, if only to affirm your competence and widen the range of your potential potence." In a subsequent letter to Séamas, Charles wrote, "You must go on writing."

Charles's close friendships with other writers demonstrated a supportive rather than competitive relationship with them, delight in their accomplishments, and desire to help them whenever he could, whether it was through encouragement, lodging, or help in bringing them recognition. He loved the intellectual stimulation they provided during long evenings of conversation at the local tavernas.

When Charles's finances began to run low, he moved to Plantanias, a village near Hania. There he was able to rent a cottage and to secure work as a translator and "mediator" for Leif Storhaug, a former Norwegian ship owner who had retired to Crete. Storhaug had entered into a business relationship with the Greek owners of the Mill Restaurant at the end of the village. In addition to his business relationship with Storhaug, Charles had borrowed money from him with his library as collateral.

During this period, Charles continued to accumulate and organize material for, in his words, "a multivolume, quasi-autobiographical novel set in Greece and Crete during two periods a century apart." The first volume of this novel continued the story of the Greek-American boy John Kallergis, whom Charles introduced in *The Sun's Attendant* as a Heidelberg student and then, in a prequel, as the newsboy protagonist of *The Snowman*. In his new novel, John Kallergis discovered and claimed his Greek identity and, after college and naval experiences mirroring those of Charles Haldeman, fulfilled his ambition to settle in Greece.

Later volumes were to be set in Greece, describing Greek events "a century apart": the great Cretan revolution of 1868 against the Ottoman Empire and the political crises plaguing Greece in the 1960s. The novel's protagonist, John Kallergis, experiencing the latter crises, was greatly affected by the writings of American consult William J. Stillman on the Cretan revolution of the 1860s, especially the heroic last stand of Crete's revolutionaries at the Arkadhi Monastery. The novel was titled *The Arkadhi Alphabet*. (Though Charles described this to his family as his "Greek" novel, only the first volume, *The Criss Cross Row*—mainly dealing with Kallergis's pre-Greek life—was ever completed.) He was to suffer another blow when Tom Maschler turned down *The Criss Cross Row* for publication.

Charles had completed his spy-mystery novel *Oracle in a Safe Place*, going against his principle of never writing a merely "popular" novel; but Tom Maschler also felt there was no market for this book. Despite the rejection of *The Criss Cross Row* by Jonathan Cape, Charles continued to revise this and to work on a future volume of *The Arkadhi Alphabet*. He was also continuing to develop the documentary on the life of Nikos Katzantzakis. His mind and typewriter remained active, but he became increasingly dependent upon others for money, food, and lodging.

The situation in Plantanias was becoming increasingly unsustainable as Séamas Carraher explained to Richard Haldeman: "There were many problems in the village, mostly tension between the locals and the 'foreigners'—and Leif, I gather, was not making things easier, constantly fighting with his business partners… Though Charles was greatly respected and liked by most in the village (not all, I think!) the disagreements between Leif and the local people put pressure on him… in all the time I had known Charles I had never seen him so stressed out."

Finally in 1979, Greek-Canadian filmmaker Henri Yatrou provided Charles an escape from his quandary. Henri had known Charles since 1960, when he worked as assistant director of *It Happened in Athens*, and now selected Charles to write the scripts for a series on the Greek communities in Canada. After preliminary interviews with Greek-Canadians in Greece, Charles moved to Montreal, where he worked from 1979 through 1981 on these documentaries.

Charles's brother Richard and his wife, Janice, can attest to the satisfaction Charles must have felt working with Henri Yatrou. Two decades later they spent a pleasant evening with Henri and his wife, Nitsa, in Montreal, with Henri regaling them with stories of working with such great producers as Cecil B. DeMille and Nitsa serving them a delicious Greek supper. Henri expressed his appreciation for Charles's work, and the Yatrous told of their pleasure in serving as his colleague and host. Charles was delighted with his "little apartment next door to Henri's…fully furnished with kitchenette (electric stove and fridge) and tiled bath and lots of closets, with water, electricity, fumigation and central heating"—all at a "quite unbelievable" low rent.

In a December 1979 letter to Séamas Carraher, Charles expressed optimism for the new decade, stating that "the 1970s were not only ghastly, they were unholy." Though he looked forward to the 1980s, he pointed out, "Actually I believe that the determining events of any ten year period occur in year number three of the decade itself—whether Stalingrad in '43; the coming of Eisenhower/Nixon and the end of the Korean War in '53, along with the reinstatement of the Shah by the C.I.A.; the assassination of Kennedy and the reopening of the Cyprus wound in '63; Watergate and the oil crisis in '73…but it will be nice nonetheless to start writing that 'eight.'" (Ironically, Charles's life was to come to an end in '83.)

"We must not only endure, we must prevail," Charles continued, "and I've only started, in the past few years, to grasp the implications of survival plus, or survival for…Nothing we have done or been up to a given moment in our lives has the least significance except in what we do or are from then on."

The 1979–81 years provided Charles the opportunity for his first extended visit to the United States in five years and the opportunity to travel throughout the nation. In April 1980, he wrote Séamas, "I just got back to Canada yesterday after almost two & a half months in the States & about 9,000 miles of travel." Montreal's proximity to the northern New York state enabled him to spend time in Sackets Harbor for the first time in more than three decades. This trip was made with his parents, and while in northern New York, he and they were reunited with family friend Florence Louth, now retired. Montreal was also close to Michigan, and Charles several times visited his brother Neil, whose family now included a baby son, in Ann Arbor. He also made several trips to New York City, where he visited friends and his brother Jim, stationed with the Coast Guard on Governor's Island. Séamas Carraher also visited America during those years, and Charles was able to travel with him and to introduce him to Florence Louth in Clayton, New York. In a her letter to Bill Haldeman following Charles's death, Florence wrote, "Last year (1981) around the 4th of July holiday Charlie called from Montreal & was coming through with two friends, a young woman doctor, Dr. Sara Johnson, and a young man fresh from Ireland (Séamas). You could cut his Irish brogue with a knife." After Florence was their host for dinner and an evening of conversation, the group spent the night at a Clayton motel before joining her again for breakfast. They wished to rent a cottage for the Fourth of July, but nothing was available "on the St. Lawrence or Lake Ontario." Despite Charles's later calls to Florence and attempts through Dr. Sara Johnson to arrange eye surgery for her in New York, this was to be the last time Florence was to see Charles.

The previous year, 1980, Florence had been host to Charles, Frances, and Bill Haldeman while they were visiting Sackets Harbor. In her letter to Bill, she recalled Frances telling her, "Charlie was the only one [of her sons] she worried about" as he "still hasn't really settled down." Despite her closeness to Charles, Frances showed she never completely understood her son. Florence showed a deeper understanding of him in her letter to Bill: "I believe it (Charles's life) was just the way he wanted it. He was bright, independent and dedicated to doing his thing the Charles Haldeman way. I respected Charlie and cared about him."

Charles reciprocated that respect and care by attempting to find Florence the best medical care through Dr. Sara Johnson in New York. He also called upon her to provide a "real" American Thanksgiving dinner for a Greek female friend who would be visiting the United States, but Florence's health would not permit her to do so.

In correspondence with Richard Haldeman, Séamas Carraher explained how he happened to be in America at the same time as

Charles: "On his return to America Charles met with (the poet) David Levine in New York… who then began a correspondence with myself culminating in an invitation to stay with him. Charles initially was against this (he felt there was a lot of destructiveness in New York that I might well get sucked into) but then embraced it when I made the decision to travel. While working in Montreal Charles spent a good amount of time when free in New York as he knew many people there. I was lucky in that he met me at the airport and we spent about a week together while he introduced me to people there before returning to work… at that time he was encouraging me to write 'fulltime.'" In New York Séamas also struck up a friendship with Sara Johnson, who accompanied him and Charles on their visit to northern New York.

A letter from Charles to Séamas in early 1980 explained how David Levine happened to invite Séamas to America. During his "nine thousand mile" trip throughout the United States, Charles had stayed in New York City with Levine, whom he had met in Greece, and shown him a poem by Séamas. Charles wrote Séamas, "He will be writing you shortly… he is a very good & honest poet…with whom you might it profitable to correspond, at least literarily… I have not found anyone as knowledgeable as he about world poetry." Charles added, with a lament for the plight of the literary artist, "David will get some people to read your poems if you send him a selected batch, but except for a few little magazines whose quality remains high but who pay next-to-nothing, the poet has as few outlets as, or fewer than, the prose writers, in these days of print-drought & reader-death."

In New York City, Charles stayed at the apartments of Ted Whittemore and David Levine, sometimes serving as chef for them and other New York City friends. Although Ted and Carol Martin were no longer a couple, they remained friends; and Charles also renewed his friendship with Carol, who longed for more than friendship, as she revealed in a long letter to Séamas after Charles's death. "We never let ourselves say as much as we needed to one another," she said. "I hope he knew how much I loved him and love him."

During his time in America, Séamas was also able to share with Charles a visit with the artist Roger Long, Charles's friend from Navy days, in Santa Fe, New Mexico, and to meet Charles's parents in Fairhope, Alabama. He described the experience: "Charles had some time off from Radio Quebec and decided he would travel and visit some people and suggested I get out of New York for a while and meet his friend Roger Long on Don Gaspar Drive outside Santa Fe. I followed a week or two later taking the Greyhound to Albuquerque, where he and Roger picked me up. We stayed about a week or so before Charles took me to Fairhope to visit his parents. We then traveled to Juarez (for only a day as I had no money whatsoever and Charles had about 20 dollars!) and then made our way back to New York (very hungry). Charles then went to Montreal to finish out his contract with Radio Quebec."

After Charles's death, Roger Long wrote Séamas of what Charles's visit meant to him: "His death leaves a lot of things unfinished for me—not just unfinished, but unfinishable and unknowable…twelve years had elapsed— and finally there he was again with a lot of catching up to do. I had a feeling that his visit here had satisfied something in him that needed satisfying and I was looking forward to other visits that might be less intense." Perhaps what "needed satisfying" for Charles was knowledge that Roger had overcome his "self-destructive" problem with depression and alcohol and gained "freedom to get at things that are important to me." Roger urged Séamas to do the same, stating, "You and I have been in the same boat [has to do in part with self-concept?]."

These letters indicate just how much personal relationships meant to Charles Haldeman but also what intense empathy he had for his friends and how much he longed for their personal and artistic success. In another letter to Séamas, Roger Long writes of visiting and sharing memories of Charles with their Navy friend Al McCarthy "on the West Coast."

Intentionally or unintentionally, Charles was rounding out his life with visits to people and places in his past, guilty of the same sentimentality he scorned in others. How much Charles's relationships with others meant to him and to them was expressed in a letter from Séamas to Charles's dad, Bill Haldeman, following Charles's death: "I have never met a man so genuinely loved by so many people…what he stood for was life and a life worth living."

These years in America also provided Charles the opportunity to reassess his native country. He expressed his feelings toward the America in a letter to Alexandra: "I really long to be back in Greece;

not because the daily intercourse with Americans is disagreeable—quite the contrary, there is great goodness & intensity & fruitful activity & intellectual activity here—but because the diversity is so great that in the end one is deprived of all centrality in relations to the whole. Ultimately, there is no whole, no point of focus. Anything can and will be accomplished, but the object is invisible: greater and greater freedom without an aim, without the kind of discrimination that insists on values where all human values come together, even occasionally, even accidentally, and where equality is only under law and not in selfish practice." He criticized Americans' "submission to power—concentration that leaves them confused and impotent as individuals." He could well have been speaking to the America of the twenty-first century, with its polarization, concentration of economic and political power, and continued subjugation of human values.

During his time in America, he was also able to visit publishers and film producers with his novels and film scripts. Alexandra and his German friend Renate Gerhardt were also making contacts for him in Europe. Through Yatrou Productions Ltd. in Montreal, Charles had prepared and was offering to filmmakers a shooting outline and breakdown of sequences for a documentary film on Nikos Kazantzakis that he hoped would be released during that author's centennial in 1983. With Henri Yatrou he was producing several documentaries for Canadian TV (Radio Quebec) on the foreign minorities in Canada that were shown in 1981–82. He wrote Alexandra in September 1980: "I just signed a contract with Radio Quebec (TV) to do the research & writing of nine half-hour documentaries (with Henry as director) between now & next April." A month later he was able to report: "Well, the first four films are finished (one the Moslems & Arabs) and the first got raves from the official community here (in Montreal)—about 20 phone calls from professors and professional people—and no complaints from the Jewish bloc." He said that on "the first of December... we start working on the Greek series, which promises to be fun." Charles was also in touch with publishers in England and America concerning publication of his novels and said Houghton Mifflin was "still interested in *Arkadhi* and its eventual successors." He said that his prospective agent in London "likes *Oracle in a Safe House* and thinks she can sell it."

Charles remained disappointed that Tom Maschler had turned down his novels, insinuating that his commitment to Greece was blocking his creative talent. In 1980 Maschler wrote him, "You say you resent my disapproval of your commitment to Greece. Whilst it is true that I believe and have believed for a number of years that the atmosphere in Crete and especially around the house was blocking you in some way, I really don't see why this should cause resentment in you. Except in so far as your commitment to the place was so great that even if I were right, you couldn't possibly afford to admit it."

Before leaving America, Charles enjoyed a two-day sailing trip off New England with his Coast Guard brother Jim and renewed his friendship with Ted (Edward Whittemore). Ted had allowed Charles to use his apartment in New York City, where he found relief from outdoor temperatures in the nineties. Charles had recognized Ted's writing talent during their years in Hania but felt he lacked personal and literary discipline to succeed. Now he praised Ted's "real self-disciplined transformation" that had led to publication of several novels.

Charles was also able to spend time with Alexandra during his final weeks in America. She remembered, "In November 1981, I also went to New York and stayed with Charles at Carol's apartment." When Charles went on to Canada, Alexandra visited "some friends in Harvard and elsewhere in the United States…" (She mentioned famed underwater archaeologist Peter Throckmorton and his former and new wife; Dr. Freeman, a contributor to *International History Magazine,* and his wife in Philadelphia; the head of NBC ["Adams, I think"] to whom she had been introduced by a journalist friend in Greece; and her former secretary in New Hampshire.) To close her American stay, Alexandra remembered, "Peter picked me up and took me to his 17th century house in Maine, where he lived with his new wife, and from there I went on to Montreal and stayed with Charles a few weeks until we both left and went back to New York. Then I left for Greece." Charles also returned to Greece shortly thereafter, with the hope that his work in Canada had relieved him "at least partly out of the morass of debt I've fallen into during these past years" and that he would "be able to reestablish himself in Greece with a clear head." Alexandra had secured legal help for him to fight for Angel One, and he was able to resume work on *The Arkadhi Alphabet.* He had gained a new perspective on the novel, writing in his "Outline of Life in Greece": "I had too much to say to cram it into a fictional frame… If my novel was to be truthful, it would have to be drastically restricted and simplified, and 'Greece' could not be treated as the heroine in a love story, no matter how many analogies abounded."

Charles was, however, expressing his love for Greece in the Kazantzakis documentary and a film script he had prepared with Christopher Miles, which they hoped to sell to an American or British movie company. This script, *The Cretan Runner,* was based on the wartime experiences and memoir of George Psychoundakis. Although he still had to deal with his business conflicts, poverty, and debts in Plantania, Charles had regained his focus and was again able to concentrate on his writing. Then, early in 1982, shortly after returning to Greece, Charles received terrible news that was to bring him back to America. His mother had been diagnosed with terminal lung cancer.

## III

# "A Light Goes Out": The South Revisited, Final Days in Athens

Bill and Frances Haldeman had moved from Waveland, Mississippi, to Fairhope, Alabama, in 1977 following Bill's diagnosis of throat cancer and his laryngectomy that followed. They had rented an apartment next to the home of Frances's brother, Waddy McFall, now retired to Alabama following years as a taxidermist in Montana. Both Bill and Frances had been heavy smokers for decades; Frances had given up smoking during Bill's battle with cancer and operation but resumed the habit a few months later. Despite Bill's speech handicap, the couple enjoyed a happy life in this tourist haven on the Gulf of Mexico for more than four years. Bill played golf, and he and Frances made close friends and enjoyed a trip to Hawaii with Frances's brother Waddy, sister Vesta, and Waddy's wife, Evelyn.

It was in early 1982, soon after the return from the Hawaii trip, however, that Frances received the diagnosis of lung cancer. When Charles arrived in Fairhope in May 1982, the remainder of her family—her husband, four other sons, three daughters-in-law, and eight grandchildren—had already gathered there to be with Frances during her final days. Frances, bedridden but still at home, especially enjoyed the company of her six granddaughters, some now young women. She was able to say goodbye to her family before they left to resume their lives—all but Charles. Her firstborn son—whom she had reared through her widowhood, remarriage, and financial struggles— was with her during her first weeks in hospice and was the last of the sons to say goodbye to her before her death in July.

Charles found solace in his grief in this poem written by his Irish friend Séamas Carraher:

# RICHARD HALDEMAN

a light goes out
don't pause for thought
a light leaves
other halos listen
low helloes
from afar a light
in the dark in the
night listen
sleep and stumbling sighs
rise on the light
a light will listen
rise on the sound
hear where it's gone listen
a light goes out
see it! How far
afar comes closer
listen what's now
is a trick of light
there and back a
trick of touch
to steal a sense
O listen to light
what's here and there
us-All between-Us
listen and listen
hear where the light goes
here where the sigh
goes the sound of the light
of circles now far is
under-the-thumbnail
sorrow sow time see
the sound of seed sorrow
a light gone out gone
out to tomorrow listen!
A light goes out
but love, now we'll
feel it Listen!

In his final days in America, Charles spent several days with his aunt Vesta at her home in Pickens, South Carolina, where Charles was reacquainted with high school friends, and in Due West, South Carolina, where they visited his brother Richard and his family and enjoyed a pleasant afternoon with Dr. J. Mauldin Lesesne or "Tum," retired president of Erskine College, and his wife Henrietta ("Totsy"). During the visit they ate and drank from the same flatware as they had thirty-three years before, when Charles was a student and Dr. Lesesne a professor, in the same historic Due West home to which the Lesesnes had retired.

When Charles returned to Greece, he realized the bitterness in Platanias was too much for him and moved in with Lee Rediasis in Athens, in return for typing and editing a novel she was writing. She left him little time for his own writing projects. He found relief during this time through the kindness of Alexandra Fiada and her mother and other friends in Athens dating back to his years at the Anglo-American School. While attempting to write, Charles also had to deal with the conflict between the two women in his life, Alexandra and Lee. His professional relationship with Alexandra had grown into a love affair, but his need for lodging and a place to write had brought him under the control of Lee, who thought Alexandra a threat to his writing.

According to Alexandra, Lee told her, "Charles is useful to me. If you think that you are going to have him, you are very much mistaken. I can turn him round my little finger." Alexandra admitted, "Of course he had to stay with Lee and be 'useful,' since he wasn't paying any rent, and she was driving him up the wall with her crazy ways and her selfishness." While Lee provided Charles a living space, Alexandra and her mother saw that he could visit them and have a home. Alexandra also secured legal help for him to fight for ownership of Angel One. She had hired an attorney, Grigoris Bitsikokos, to represent Charles in his case for Angel One against Nikos Stavroulakis. (Following Charles's death, his brothers Richard and Neil were placed in the middle of the conflict between these women during their visit to Greece to help settle Charles's affairs.)

Shortly after returning to Greece, Charles wrote his dad, Bill Haldeman, on August 11: "I'm simply glad that the gathering of the family was possible while Mom could still muster the strength both to put up with it and, for moments, to enjoy it, especially because it included your 45th Anniversary.

"I'm also deeply grateful for your letter; I know what it must have cost you to sit down right away and let us all have the sad news, but also the reassurance that her last week was without pain. Please thank the doctor on my behalf for that, if you should see him again.

"I also want you to know how much I love you, and how fortunate I feel I have been in having you as a father... Anything I can ever, ever do or offer, in gratitude and love, just let me know."

Charles's expression of love must have brought great joy to Bill Haldeman, with whom Charles had such a difficult early childhood experience. Charles also expressed great sensitivity in letters to his father and his brother Richard to the difficulties Richard and his wife, Janice, were encountering with their teenage son Ross. He directly addressed Ross, building him up, in a letter to Richard; and in a letter to Bill Haldeman, he asked, "How is Ross getting along? He seemed so much more stable & mature this summer; if he could manage to lose some weight, it would provide an even further boost to his morale." Sadly, Ross never completely overcame his problems and, like his uncle Charlie, lived a short life.

Whether intentionally or not, Charles Haldeman was finding peace in the turmoil of his life. This even extended to, as he expressed it in his "Outline of Life in Greece," his "marriage for good or ill, to a country." He had begun to "redesign, as far as I could, the novel I would write when I had either won or lost the battle for my house, and the reassessment was complete, either in divorce or reconciliation."

During this time, Alexandra remembered a deepening of her relationship with Charles: "Charles and I were at a party...in the northern suburbs of Athens, where we had a great time. Actually, on the way there, in the trolley-bus, a very correct gentleman gave me his seat, since I was wearing a rather voluminous velvet coat and he thought I must be pregnant. Charles's comment was: 'We should get married soon, if we wish for a couple of kids—sometime in the spring?' And we laughed. (Afterward I was told by my mother that, as she was leaving for Christmas in South Africa with her sister's family, that Charles [who had insisted at accompanying us to the airport] had told her not to tarry too long in S. A. since he wanted to talk to her.)"

Charles's deep relationship with Alexandra—personal and professional— and his many friendships in Athens relieved his anxieties concerning his writing and litigation over Angel One. On December 5, he wrote his father Bill Haldeman concerning the status of both his writing and litigation: "I wanted to be able to announce that my film of George Psychoundakis's *Cretan Runner* was going to be made, and that all my work over the past year, since leaving Canada, had finally paid off. But it's still hanging fire, though the outlook remains good & I'm expecting positive news from London any day now. Christopher Miles (with whom, by the way, Mom got the chance to speak on the phone during the week you were away, when he called me from Hollywood) has been out to Greece three times during the past five months, and we have developed what I think is a very fine scenario. Let's hope the producers he is showing it to think so as well!

"The next hearing on the house-case is January 25th, so I'll be going down (to Hania) for that—but unless Christopher comes through on the film before that, I'll be here in Athens (at Lee's) straight through." Charles could not have realized the irony of those words nor those in the final paragraph of the letter: "Don't worry about me. My health is excellent & I'm working with high hopes."

Those "high hopes" had to mask deep stress caused by lack of funds and financial dependence on friends; his father, Bill; and brother Neil. The "excellent" health was undermined by a diet deficient in amount and overly dependent on alcohol. During their time with Charles, his brothers noted that Charles ate small portions, keeping himself very slim, but continually sipped wine while working or in conversation. In his final letter to Bill Haldeman, Charles thanked his father for funds, and Neil loaned him money several times.

Alexandra remembered Charles enjoying a very happy Christmas with her, her mother, and their Greek friends. In the New Year, he began sorting out his papers in preparation for moving out from Lee's and worked with Alexandra and his attorney, Grigoris Bitsikokos, on the approaching court hearing on Angel One, scheduled for January 25. Though he became ill Sunday, January 16, and discovered blood in his stools, Charles refused to go to the hospital and continued to plan for this hearing. Though still very ill and weak two days later, Tuesday, January 18, Charles asked Alexandra to "negotiate with the owner of the apartment that we had inspected in the next street…so that we could start moving into it after we came back from Crete (from the hearing on Angel One). Also to go and pick up the tickets for flying to Chania on Friday and, further, that on Thursday evening we would go to the cinema to see Annie."

At 2:00 a.m. on January 19, 1983, only hours after Charles and Alexandra made those ill-fated plans, the telephone rang at Neil Haldeman's home in Ann Arbor, Michigan. In his unpublished memoir, *The Difficulty of Dying in Greece,* Neil recalled, "In my heavy sleep I didn't even hear the phone ring that night in January, 1983. My wife, Ruth, came across our dark bedroom, her bare heels pounding on the carpeted wood floor, saying loudly, 'Neil…it's a long-distance phone-call.' I…picked the phone up off the table where Ruth had left it, and said, 'Hello.'

"'Hello, Neil,' the voice said. 'Neil, this is Lee, in Athens…' The connection was very bad. It came out more like, 'Neil…is Lee… Athens.' I would not have recognized the name without the place. But the combination of Lee and Athens was enough to let me know this was about Charlie. 'Neil…afraid…very bad news. Charles…and died…morn…' I said nothing. I was considering, I think, whether I had heard correctly, when Lee continued, '…connect…bad…will call ba…' and the line went dead."

Neil continued, "When the phone call came in 1983, it turned into the worst night of my life. Lee did call back in a few minutes, on a good line. And I had heard correctly… She didn't say it, but I knew that the reason I, the youngest brother, was chosen for the notification was simply that my name would have been the one Lee had heard most recently." Six hours after the telephone call, a telegram arrived from the American Embassy in Athens, informing the family (through Neil) of Charles's death and the need to make a decision regarding interment "within 24 hours." To the everlasting gratitude of the Haldeman family, Alexandra Fiada "came to the rescue…it was arranged that Charlie would be buried in the Fiada family plot in Athens." Letters from Lee and Alexandra described Charles's death. Lee wrote:

> On Monday, the 17th (of January) he (Charles) told me he had had, during the (previous) night, severe vomiting and diarrhea with blood in his stool… He said he felt perfectly

well, but I called my doctor and let them talk together on the telephone. At his suggestion, Charles promised to visit him that evening. I took the doctor's instructions on diet and a light stomach easing medicine.

Charles spent the day Monday in bed reading and talking with visitors and insisting that he felt no pain nor discomfort. By the evening, however, he said he felt too tired to go to the doctor and would put it off until the following day, Tuesday. I phoned the doctor and they spoke together again, Charles saying he would visit him the next day.

On Tuesday Charles continued to appear perfectly well but said he was too tired to hang around waiting in doctors' offices. I arranged with my doctor to call him at 7:45 on Wednesday morning so that if Charles were not regaining strength he could visit him on his way to his hospital nearby.

I was awoken in the middle of the night by extraneous sounds and went to check on Charles. Getting no answer when I knocked on the door gently, I looked in and saw the bed empty. The door of the bathroom (just beside the bed) was open and the light there was on. Thinking he had been taken with more bowel trouble, I waited a few moments and then called out. Getting no answer, I went in and found him lying unconscious on the bathroom floor... Finding no response, I called Alexandra (who lives next door almost) and asked her to come and help.

Lee told Alexandra that she had "called her doctor, who would be coming over."

Alexandra wrote that on her arrival, "I ran to the bathroom of the adjoining Papadakis' apartment and Charles was there, lying on the tiles stark naked... He was not cold yet, but I took my mirror and held it under his nose. Nothing! The doctor arrived, tried resuscitation and gave him a shot at the heart, but to no avail. He pronounced him dead... I said, 'Doctor, please help me put him on his bed.' And together we lifted Charles's body." Alexandra then "called my friend Heracles Dimopoulos, who lived on the flat above mine with his wife, and who was a doctor... He came in, and filled the necessary papers, saying that Charles had died of a perforated ulcer. Lee called the American Embassy and they dispatched the best undertaker of Athens to the house. I had to deal with them, find some wine, so that they would wash the body (as is the tradition) find his clothes and good suit (which I had bought for him at Harrods) and lay him out. They took him away, awaiting further instructions, and told me that they would take the casket to the First Athens Cemetery.

"I called my aunt Antonia, to ask her whether she would have any objection to have Charles buried in our family plot in Piraeus. She was devastated, said 'Of course not' and went ahead and called my mother in South Africa. Half an hour later, my mother called me at Lee's to tell me that she was flying in as soon as possible (it took her 19 hours, because she had to come via Lisbon), and my uncle Charalambos told me to take any money I would be needing for the funeral from his account in Athens."

Charles Haldeman died early in the morning of Wednesday, January 19, 1983, homeless and penniless. Charles had chosen Greece as a home and lived there the final half of his fifty-one years. Though never accepted as a Greek citizen, he now makes his final home in Greek soil through the love of Alexandra Fiada, one of a myriad of Greek friends. Identifying herself as Charles's fiancée, Alexandra was able to secure permission for his burial in her family plot in Athens. Burial took place on January 22 with many of Charles's friends in attendance.

Alexandra described Charles's funeral in a letter to Neil Haldeman, written January 25, 1983—ironically, the date on which the litigation on Angel One had been scheduled. She wrote:

> I made all the arrangements in the best possible way. His casket was very simple, of solid oak with bronze handles. It was filled with white spring flowers (I think they are called jonquils) and the lid was covered with red and white roses, plus all the other flowers his friends brought. Charles looked as peaceful and handsome as if he was asleep.
>
> The funeral service was held at the Greek Orthodox Church, and it was performed by two priests and byzantine singers—it is a very moving ceremony, if one understands the language. Many of his friends were there—every single one looking

absolutely shattered and crying—and twice as many were unable to come because simply they couldn't face it.

After the burial in our family grave, we all went for the traditional Greek coffee and brandy, and after that all his close friends went to "Seventeen" and had a few drinks—after all it was Saturday, and every Saturday Charles and I used to meet our friends there and drink and talk late into the afternoon.

Afterward I went back to my house, where all my family had gathered, and we had a second wake with lots of wine until well after midnight.

A month after Charles Haldeman's death, Neil and Richard Haldeman traveled to Greece to attend a Greek Orthodox memorial mass for him, meet his myriad of friends at a reception, and help settle his literary estate. (This was later accomplished through Peter Levi, who also edited Charles's book of poems and wrote a memorial poem in Charles's honor in the poetry periodical Agenda.) While in Athens, the Haldeman brothers were caught between two strong women—Lee Rediadis and Alexandra Fiada—each claiming to represent Charles and work in his interest.

Neil and Richard owed much to each woman. Lee had provided Charles a place to live, write, and store his manuscripts and books. Alexandra had provided him love, literary help, a home where he could relax, and a place of burial. She and her mother were also wonderful hosts to the brothers during their time in Athens, providing home-cooked meals. Alexandra also urged the brothers to continue the litigation over Angel One. (The four living Haldeman brothers did provide funds for this, though the case was postponed and then lost.)

Though Alexandra had arranged the burial, the brothers faced many other problems: finalizing the litigation over Angel One, selecting a legal power of attorney and a literary executor for Charles and distinguishing between the two, settling all affairs with the consulate in Athens, and satisfying the differences between Alexandra Fiada and Lee Rediasis over how things should be done.

Eventually, everything was settled. Alexandra assumed Charles's power of attorney, and Charles's lawyer friend, Grigoris Bitsikokos, was retained to continue the litigation over the house. Peter Levi accepted Lee's request to serve as literary executor. Neil and Richard visited the embassy to clear all remaining bureaucratic hurdles. They also had rewarding telephone conversations with Tom Maschler and Christopher Miles.

With Alexandra as their hostess, Neil and Richard enjoyed their remaining time in Athens, attending the memorial service, visiting ancient Hellenic sites, eating delicious meals in the Fiada home and in local restaurants, and meeting and sharing pleasant hours with Charles's friends. Neil Haldeman described this experience in *The Difficulty of Dying in Greece:*

> On Sunday we went to the memorial service that Alexandra had arranged and stood in the back of the Greek Orthodox church amidst incense and candles and chanting while several priests performed their circular parade-like rituals in the small back room, feeling as if we had accidentally wandered into the filming of a Kazantzakis novel. But afterward, there was a pleasant gathering of Charlie's friends in another building, where we had ouzo and brandy and coffee, bread and cheese and cakes.
>
> Among the friends were Louis Hepp, who had been NBC's chief of European operations at one time, Basil Maros, who had collaborated with Charlie on several documentary films, and George Poulos, who owned the "17," an American bar known for its famous clientele, and where Charlie had probably bent elbows with Alan Ginsburg and Gore Vidal and Elia Kazan at one time or another. Later in the week we would have dinner at Louis Hepp's home and lunch downtown with George Poulos.

At the reception following the memorial service, Alexandra Hionides, the widow of Charles's friend and former colleague Harry Hionides, summed up the sentiment of Charles's Greek friends. She said, "Greece has lost a hero."

# PART NINE

# "It's Life That Matters"
# (Dostoyevsky, The Idiot)

## I

# A WORLD LONG PASSED; VISION OF A HIGHER GOOD

Charles would have appreciated Alexandra Hionides's remark, showing recognition by many Greek people, if not the Greek government, that Greece was his home. In truth, however, Charles Haldeman never "belonged" to a country or a place. A college professor of Richard Haldeman's daughter Nancy, after reading *The Sun's Attendant,* told her, "Your uncle's plane landed everywhere." Charles had indeed lived throughout the United States and in Germany, Greece, and Canada; traveled throughout Europe and in the Middle East; and while in the Navy, visited the Far East.

Charles did, however, belong to a "time." A child of the Depression and World War II who grew to adulthood in the 1950s, Charles Haldeman chronicled the world of his time in three novels and found early success as a writer of fiction and documentaries, only to find interest in midcentury America and Europe and print media fade in a time of the Cold War, racial unrest, assassinations, Eastern and Middle Eastern wars, and the dawning of the information age. His last published novel failed to find an audience, and his final two novels and several film scripts were unsuccessful in securing a publisher or producer.

As Séamas Carraher pointed out to Charles's brother Richard, Charles's generation lived in "a world long passed...not just the century, but its taste and feel and everything that gave it body... We live in a very different world today." But Richard and others of that now-shrinking generation realize that today's "very different world" was molded by events in that "world long passed," with its hot and cold wars; ideological, religious, and racial revolutions; collapse of colonialism and Soviet communism; and development of weapons of mass destruction.

Those events were the genesis of troubles today in North Korea, Iran, Russia, Iraq, Afghanistan, and Central and South America and of the rejuvenation of nationalism and fascism throughout the world. Charles Haldeman was a member of the "forgotten," often too-silent generation born in the 1930s, in the notch between the wartime "Great" generation and its children, the baby boomers. He grew up during the Great Depression, Second World War, the Korean Conflict, and the Cold War. As a writer, he was able to describe this time and his generation as a witness, providing the "taste and body" of his era. His was the final generation (before television and the computer) in which the written word, newspapers, magazines, books, and even letters, had prime importance.

Charles also gained the love and respect of his generation's writers and artists—British, American, German, Irish, and Greek. Deprived by fate of the means and education of most accomplished writers, he educated himself and became their peer. Better still, he was their host and their friend, offering them artistic stimulation and encouragement rather than competition. As his friend Peter Levi wrote in his introduction to Charles's posthumously published book of poems *without graves, no resurrections:* "If Charles had not existed, one might have invented him, plucked him from the air and darkness…"

Yet his letters, his novels, and all his other manuscripts fail to capture the essence of who Charles Haldeman was. It was something perhaps he himself never understood, though he tried to explain himself in his letters to his mother. There was duplicity even in his name. Charles's drawings and writings, including an article in *The International History Magazine* and an unpublished novel, are sometimes ascribed to "Charles Heuss," his birth name and that of his birth father. Ironically, Charles had the concentration camp philosopher in *The Sun's Attendant* describe maintaining one's identity as the core of one's existence.

As a man and as a writer, Charles lacked a "sense of place." Was he an American…a German…a Greek? If an American, was he a Southerner, a New Yorker, or a Californian? How could he claim to love America but find it impossible to live there? After rejecting America for its materialism, lack of values, and failure to carry out its ideals and Germany for its emptiness of purpose, could he recreate himself as a Greek, living among a people whose freedom he admired? And how would a settled life in Greece affect the creative talents of this wandering artist? Strangely, it was an American, Stavroulakis, who caused Charles to fail in his effort to become Greek, who was successful in recreating himself as a Greek and an Israeli.

Was Charles Haldeman a failure as a writer? That he is still being read today, through publication of his first novel in Germany more than thirty years after his death, attests to his novels still having something to say. Even if, as Tom Maschler expressed in a telephone call with Richard Haldeman in 1983, he had failed to fulfill the promise of his first two novels, Charles was embarked on resurrecting his life and career. He was convinced that, as he wrote Séamas Carraher, he would not only "endure" but also "prevail."

Neil Haldeman perhaps best expressed Charles's difficulty in finding an audience for his fiction. He wrote in *The Difficulty of Dying in Greece,* "He (Charles) chose to become a novelist and achieved some early success at it, largely due to his friendship with Tom Maschler, but his work was so abstract, so complex, that only a truly dedicated reader could absorb it. Those readers would be rewarded in the end; but Charlie probably never would have acquired much of an audience in America."

Was Charles's life a tragedy? In his early death and failure to fulfill completely his literary and personal dreams, perhaps. But not in living a full life, however short, filled with hundreds of friends in Greece, America, Germany, England, Ireland, and wherever he had traveled. Séamas expressed to Richard how closely the message of Charles's novels was integrated with his life: "As opposed to seeking fame or money, Charles always had a vision of a higher good that he sought to unearth and give voice to." Séamas told Richard of his last telephone conversation with Charles in early January 1983: "He sounded his own strong optimistic self with hopes and plans plentiful for a future filled with creativity, work, and intense relationships, along with the unfolding of the many questions about the meaning of our lives he had carried with him since his youth." (When he read these words from Séamas, Richard was reminded of how moved Charles had been at the age of sixteen, watching the film *The Razor's Edge,* whose protagonist sought life's meaning.)

Though Charles had told his mother at the beginning of his career that his writing would never leave him time to marry, he shared intense loving relationships with his female friends. These included Caroline Aubrey, Renate Gerhardt, Carol Martin, and Alexandra Fiada; and he was discussing marriage with Alexandra just before his death.

Charles Haldeman's complexity may have been best expressed by Fyodor Dostoyevsky in his novel *The Idiot:* "There is something at the bottom of every new human thought, every thought of genius, or even every earnest thought that springs up in any brain, which can never be communicated to others…with it you will die, without communicating to anyone perhaps the most important of your ideas."

Charles Haldeman set out on a voyage of discovery, and like Odysseus, he landed on many islands along the way. That he died short of his destination "without communicating …the most important of (his) ideas" does not diminish the accomplishments of the voyage. As Dostoyevsky points out in *The Idiot,* "It's life that matters, nothing but life—the process of discovering, the everlasting and perpetual process, not the discovery itself, at all." Charles Haldeman lived; he was truly alive.

# EPILOGUE

Neil Haldeman's memoir, *The Difficulty of Dying in Greece,* describes in detail the time of Charles's death and his and Richard's experiences afterward in Greece, with flashbacks to his own relationship with Charles, closer than that of any other brother as an adult. Neil kept a diary of these events and later conducted a correspondence with Nikos Stavroulakis, who asserted his side of the Angel One controversy.

Neil's memoir was never published. Charles Haldeman's novels were long out of print, and his voluminous correspondence and unpublished novels and film scripts lay dormant for decades in the homes of Neil and Richard Haldeman. Unknown to either brother, Dr. Martin Meyer, a German professor-author, had read *The Sun's Attendant* and included a section on this novel in his 1994 book on postwar Germany as mirrored in the American novel.

In 2009 Richard Haldeman read a review of Charles's second novel, *The Snowman,* on the Neglected Books website. The Neglected Books blog roused Richard to send a reply.

One respondent to the blog reported that Charles's library had been found, strewn along a Cretan highway. Richard's response included a brief biography of Charles and explanation of where these discarded books had come from. He responded to the review with information about Charles, his life, and his works.

On reading this blog, Dr. Martin Meyer contacted Richard, and the two began a long email correspondence during which they discussed why *The Sun's Attendant* was never published in Germany. Dr. Meyer commented that one of the chief reasons no longer existed: while Germans in the 1960s were not interested in books on the wartime and immediate postwar era, Germans in the current generation desired to learn of this era.

Dr. Meyer helped bring the novel to the attention of a German publisher, Metrolit, which asked permission to translate and publish *The Sun's Attendant*. Richard Haldeman obtained the rights from the original publisher, and in 2015, the book was published in Germany as *Der Sonnen Wächter* with a *nachwort* ("afterword") by Martin Meyer. Charles's friend from his Heidelberg days, the artist Pieter Sohl, spoke of Charles at the Frankfurt Book Fair. Fifty-two years after its original publication, Charles Haldeman's first novel received outstanding reviews that brought him renewed attention thirty-two years after his death.

Dr. Meyer and Heidelberg archivist Dagmar Druell-Zimmerman also arranged for Charles Haldeman's papers to be stored in the Heidelberg University Archives. Richard and Janice Haldeman visited Germany in the summer of 2016 with Richard speaking to Martin Meyer's class at Martin Luther University in Halle on "The Legacy of Charles Haldeman." Dr. Druell-Zimmerman and her husband were hosts to Richard and Janice at a dinner in their home near Heidelberg, and Richard and Janice also enjoyed a beautiful afternoon with Charles's artist friend Pieter Sohl and his wife at their home in the Kohlhof. Richard was fortunate to hear Pieter's memories of Charles two years before Pieter himself died in 2018.

Before sending Charles's letters and manuscripts to the Heidelberg Archives, Richard had taken notes from and made copies of these materials. He and Neil also had reams of additional correspondence from Charles's family and friends telling of his last years and death. Years before, he, Neil, and Alexandra had discussed how these materials might be used in a publication. For more than two decades, this discussion remained on Richard's mind as the papers lay dormant in a vacant room while work, family responsibilities and deaths, and retirement and grandparent duties occupied his time.

After visiting Germany, Richard realized that if these materials were to be utilized, it was his responsibility. Most of Charles's contemporaries were now deceased and Richard himself was in his eighties, already living longer than most male members of his family. Only he could tell the story of Charles's birth father and his family in Germany. Only he shared and remembered Charles's childhood. He began extending a memoir he had prepared for his family of Charles's life in the 1930s and

1940s into one including Charles's adult years. To do so he depended upon Charles's correspondence with family and friends, supplemented by materials from Charles's younger friends, Séamas Carraher and Alexandra Fiada, and his brother, Neil Haldeman. Though the youngest brother, Neil shared the closest relationship with Charles.

With special help from Séamas, who took time from his own busy life as a writer to send much additional information and correspondence, Richard has compiled this memoir in memory of his brother and as an aid to future biographers of Charles Haldeman.

# ADDENDUM: CHARLES HEUSS HALDEMAN

Born September 27, 1931 (Pickens, South Carolina, USA) Died January 19, 1983 (Athens, Greece)

**Novels**

*The Sun's Attendant* (1963), published in fourteen countries

*The Snowman* (1965), published in England and the USA

*Teagarden's Gang* (1971), published in England

**Unpublished Novels**

*Oracle in a Safe House*

*The Arkadhi Trilogy or Criss Cross Row* (unfinished)

**Scriptwriter for Documentary Films**

Shown on Greek and British TV:

*The World of Icons,* film by Basil Maros, 1971; first prize at Salonika Film Festival

*New Roads,* film by Basil Maros, 1972

*Bouzouki,* film by Basil Maros, 1974

**Shown on Canadian TV (Radio Quebec):**

*Foreign Minorities in Canada,* film series by Henri Yatrou (1981–82)

Many other unproduced scripts for documentary and feature films

**Photo by Carol Martin**

**Musical Play, Book, and Lyrics**
*The Golden Wings,* performed in 1973 at Ancient Theater of Piraeus, with music by Vassilia Dimitriou

**Feature Film Lyricist**
Lyrics for title song of Twentieth Century Fox film *It Happened in Athens*(1962), with music by Manos Hadjidakis

**Editor**
*International History Magazine,* published 1973–75; Lausanne, Switzerland

**Poetry**
*without graves, no resurrections,* published posthumously in 1984 by Five Seasons Press, Madley, Hereford, England, with foreword by Peter Levi.

Parents of Charles Heuss Haldeman: Frances McFall and Charles Heuss, at time of their marriage in 1930.

Charles Haldeman's "Oma" (German grandmother) Katharina Heuss.

Charlie and Dicky Heuss at 1938 wedding in Pickens, SC, where they lived from 1936-38 after their 1936 return from Germany.

Baby Charles in 1932 with Frank McFall, his grandfather and surrogate father.

Willard W. "Bill" Haldeman, "Dad," stepfather of Charles and
Richard Haldeman.

Charles Haldeman as Boy Scout in Sackets Harbor, NY. While living in Sackets Harbor from 1942-47, Charles was chosen to deliver the Gettysburg Address on Memorial Day, delivered newspapers to 140 customers, and wrote and directed a review in which most of the town's children performed.

The Haldeman family was complete with five boys when Neil was born in 1943. From the left are Jim, Richard, Neil, Charles, and Bill, Jr. Frances Haldeman never had the daughter she coveted.

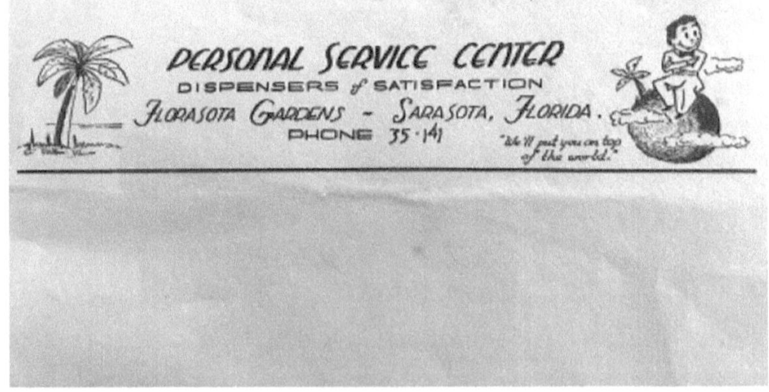


Masthead for Bill and Frances Haldeman's "Personal Service Center" in Sarasota, FL. Failure of the business caused Charles Haldeman to leave college and join the Navy.

Charles Haldeman at 17, attended Erskine College, Due West, SC, moved to Sarasota, FL, 1949

Charles Haldeman at sea, sailing out of San Diego, CA, 1953.

Charles Haldeman plays with young cousin Joerg Heuss at home of his Uncle Richard and Aunt Margarete "Grete" Heuss in Karlruhe, Germany, 1955.

Charles Haldeman at Heidelberg swimming pool with friends Roman and Francoise', 1957

Charles Haldeman with Greek friend Christos, with whom he traveled through Greece, 1956

Pen and ink drawing by Charles Haldeman, "Spiros finds a pearl,"
part of his set of 1957 Athens, Greek street scenes.

Grave of Charles Haldeman in Athens, Greece.

# ABOUT THE AUTHOR

Richard H. Haldeman grew up as next younger brother of Charles Haldeman, with whom he shared nine family relocations before Charles entered the Navy in 1950. Richard graduated from high school in Columbus, Georgia, where he won city and state journalism awards, and from Rollins College in Winter Park, Florida, where he edited the all-American student newspaper. After working as a reporter for daily newspapers in Columbus, Georgia, and Orlando, Florida, he earned a master's degree in English from George Peabody College of Vanderbilt University and taught English in Orange County, Florida, schools. He currently lives in Due West, South Carolina, where he served for thirty-four years as director of public relations for Erskine College and his wife, Dr. Janice H. Haldeman, was named professor emerita of biology in 2002. She continues to teach for the fifty-eighth year. As Erskine public relations director, Richard Haldeman wrote for and edited all publications. He continues to contribute articles to local media and college publications and has published articles in South Carolina historical magazines. Richard and Janice Haldeman are parents of two daughters—Robin Talbot of Beverly, Massachusetts, and Nancy Cochran of Powell, Tennessee—and of a deceased son, Ross. They have two grandsons, William Talbot of Wooster, MA, and Erzhan Cochran of Fort Worth, TX, both of whom have completed master's degrees and begun their careers. This memoir of Richard's brother and family fulfills his long-held desire to share memories of a unique man, family, and time.